SPLITTING SECONDS

Jackson Haime

Copyright © 2024 Jackson Haime

All rights reserved.

ISBN: 9798325376313
ISBN-13:

To my parents, who have listened to me talk about this book for the past nine years.
To my brother, Jake, who has been with me every step of the way.
And to Nick, Cameron, Robert, Jeremy, and Andrew for keeping my writing spirit alive.

1
Toby - Blind Dates

It candidly sucked being surrounded by constant reminders that you'd lost the genetic lottery. Sure, it was easier than some people thought to get around the world without powers; it wasn't like the government expected everyone to be a speedster or to be able to fly. Hell, a hundred years ago, nobody even had powers. The infrastructure was there. Life went on.

That said, staying cheery about the hand I'd been dealt was difficult. Enhanced perception was useful for a lot of things, from party tricks to always reading the fine print, but next to flight? Next to teleportation?

I'd gotten hung up on movement powers because I'd taken the bus to the bar, and the only superpower buses had was being late.

I was specifically at the bar for the sake of a blind date set up by my best friend; Todd was about two times my size and could throw a car across the street. His powers did nothing to help me with his current obsession with my dating life, but here we were. I supposed it was a fair obsession. I hadn't been trying.

It honestly made sense that Todd had been keenly aware of romance since he'd met his soulmate. See, a strange thing with powers was that when you were around your soulmate, they were inexplicably stronger. Todd had met Soo-jung when she'd been on vacation in Crescent three years ago. They'd been inseparable since, and he'd been able to throw a car down three blocks instead of across the street.

Or so he claimed. Nobody was eager to volunteer their car for a demonstration, or anything else heavy and expensive, for that matter.

For my part, I hadn't spent a lot of time guessing what would happen if I met my soulmate. It was a common train of thought for some, but I never found that it stopped at any fun stations. Instead, I indulged Todd's meddling because he was my friend and bad dates at least made good stories.

"Gimme a sec, I'll grab us another round," Todd announced as he pushed out from our table. "Emma said she's going to be here soon."

"You bought the last one."

"Yeah, now you can buy two in a row once Emma gets here and look generous. Think about it, man."

"Sure," I answered, but Todd was already walking away from the table and toward the bar.

Soo-jung leaned in. "You know he's trying, right?"

"I know, maybe a little too much."

"You don't hear the half of it."

"Oh, good."

"I had to tell him to calm down when it came to buttering you up to Emma," Soo-jung explained as she took a sip from her drink. "Sometimes I wonder about him."

"I'm surprised he says anything nice about me."

"He'd never say it to your face." She watched Todd at the bar instead of looking at me during our conversation.

"Does that mean you'll do it for him?"

"He trusts me to keep his secrets."

"How about I suggest things and read your reaction?" I asked.

Soo-jung frowned in response before she pointedly rolled her eyes. She knew that reading reactions was one of my party tricks. If you couldn't be powerful, you could at least read a room.

"Okay, fine. What do you know about Emma?"

"Her last name's Tavish," she said.

"That's it?"

"She works with Todd."

"I knew that. He kept telling me she was a coworker."

"Todd thinks she's cute."

"He told you that?" I asked.

"No, but he has high standards for you."

"That's all the detail you have?"

"Todd's not allowed to talk about work at hom-Hey, honey."

Todd was back at the table holding all three pints in one toned arm; he passed one to each of us despite Soo being less than halfway through her current drink. Once he'd finished distributing, he turned to Soo-jung and asked her a question in broken Korean.

He'd been trying to learn, and he was still struggling. Not that I knew the language.

"Yes," Soo-jung responded in English, "we were talking about Emma; no Korean around Toby. It's rude."

"I thought you wanted me to practice?"

"You can practice at home."

"So we were talking about Emma," Todd jumped back to the previous topic instead of discussing his inconsistent study of Korean. "Awesome woman, perfect for you, man."

"What makes you say that?" I asked.

"Oh, she sucks too."

"Ah, thanks."

"He means powers-wise," Soo-jung stepped in.

"So you do know something about her," I pointed out.

"Something? I've been telling Soo everything since we got in the car to come here." Just as Todd finished, he flinched. Soo had kicked him under the table. "But it wasn't much, really."

"What do I get to know?"

"I don't want to taint your expectations." He pushed his empty glass away, swapping it with the new one. "But can I be serious for a second?"

I considered it. "Sure."

"Emma's like my boss' boss' boss. So best behavior."

"Wait. Seriously?" I leaned in. Todd worked for the CPRU, which meant that she had to be a heavy hitter if she was high ranked in the city's power regulation department. "She's—"

"Not quite." He backpedaled. "We share a building. She's straight DPR."

I blinked twice at that. "Way to set me up to fail."

"You should believe in yourself," Soo cut in.

"Todd I w—"

"And she's here." Todd had turned his attention away from me and toward his phone. "Hope you're ready to meet your soulmate."

"Honey, don't set that expectation."

The bar's front door opened, and I was the only one who could hear it over the atmosphere. I glanced over, and there she was.

She was stunning by any definition, but especially mine. Maybe it was a strange way to describe someone, but she looked beautifully meticulous, from brunette hair to olive skin, to her light blue jacket; everything was in place, and everything about her was gorgeous. Assuming that was Emma, I owed Todd big time.

"Okay, that can't be her, right?" I asked Todd. After a second, without a response, I checked to see if he was waving at her, but he was stock still, a stupid grin plastered over his face. "Todd?"

Holy shit. The DPR had some crazy people on their roster, but this—I waved a hand in front of Todd's face and snapped my fingers, then caught the sound of a single cautious heel clicking against the floor.

I stood up from the table and looked back at the door. She'd taken one step into the bar but had gotten caught in the same shock I had. "Emma?" I asked.

She snapped her attention to me—god, her eyes were—but she just looked confused.

"Toby," I explained, "I'm Todd's friend." I motioned over to Todd's still body and took the first steps to say hello. "This is really impressive. I didn't think this was possible. It's cool to meet someone wh—"

"I'm not doing this," she said. "This is impossible. How are yo—"

"Trust me, this isn't in my..." We stared at each other for a moment. Somehow, time stopped more than it already was.

"Holy shit." We both said it at once.

"So this isn't you?" she asked. Her eyes were still meandering around the frozen bar instead of staying in the conversation with me.

"No, it's not." I walked along her gaze and ended up against the bar counter. "Did Todd tell you what my power was?"

"He just told me you wouldn't mind having me around," Emma answered, which somehow just brought up more questions.

"Enhanced perception." I grabbed a drink off of the bar to see if I could; as soon as I touched it, it seemed to animate back to life. "What do you mean, 'mind having you around'?"

"I dampen powers," she explained, a little quieter than anything else she'd said, "make them weaker, hard to use. The technical definition is long and wordy so..." She sighed as she watched me slosh the beer around. "It's a lot of trouble, really."

"Probably good for work," I offered.

"Pretty much the whole reason I have my job, but Callum wouldn't admit that." She approached, but there wasn't an open seat near where I was standing, nor could we ask for someone to move. "Callum is—"

"Callum Rehsman, head of the D.P.R for the past six years," I stepped in, "sorry, comes with the perception thing."

"Honestly, I'm just glad I don't have to explain it." Emma took to leaning against the bar instead of walking over to a seat. She undid the top button of her shirt, which was probably too high for a date, anyway. "Emma Terish. Ring any bells up there?"

"No."

"And you're?"

"Toby Vander." I put down the beer to offer my hand, and it

froze as soon as I let go. We both paid attention to that instead of the potential formal hello.

"So this isn't you." Emma reached for the glass and picked it up; once she did, it animated just like it had with me. "And it isn't me..."

A lump formed in my throat. We'd both said holy shit for a reason, but it felt impossible to admit it. Wasn't there supposed to be a—Well, something? Anything?

Then again, we were stopping time, and what else could you ask for?

"Do you want a drink, Toby?" Emma asked. She vaulted herself over the bar with a frankly shocking amount of grace for someone in a pantsuit.

"Uh, sure."

"I'd ask what you were drinking, but we might have limited options," she was considering her new vantage point from behind the counter.

I took the opportunity to grab the drink I'd left behind on the table. "I'll use the one I had." I tapped Todd's hand for posterity, and nothing happened to him. "Any idea what this might—"

"No idea," she answered without letting me finish, "but my job involves dealing with unknown powers, so..." She tried to use the soda-gun and swore when it didn't work. "You learn to roll with it until people cooperate."

"You still think I'm doing this?"

"I know it's not me, and there aren't many options here with us," she said as she ducked behind the bar and came back up with a lemonade cooler, "but I came here for a date, and I plan to have one. Been a long week."

I returned to the bar, finding a seat now that she was on the other side. "I just need to establish that this isn't me. I'm not trying to—"

"If it isn't you and it's not me stopping time around us, then someone is giving us a very private venue for our first date."

"Isn't that nice?"

"It really is." She took a sip of her drink, then pulled it away before she had time to swallow. "Shit. Do you have cash?"

"I'll cover you." She frowned at that; clearly she wasn't satisfied with someone else paying for everything. "Plus, you're serving me tonight. So..." That seemed to be enough plausible deniability to satisfy her. "Cheers?"

"Cheers."

Throughout drink one, we were casting nervous glances around the paused bar; by drink five, we were laughing, just the two of us. Hours dripped by with the free beer... or they didn't... It was hard to tell.

Emma added her sixth can to her pyramid and composed herself. "Okay, okay, okay. One second." She took a deep breath. "This has been so much fun, but I told Todd I'd tell him when I got here, so,"—she needed another second to find her verbal footing—"can you stop this now?"

"Stop what?" I was halfway through a sip.

"This is the coolest power I've seen but—"

"It's not me, I promise," my insistence ended up sounding more like a drunk debate. The drunk part was accurate.

"So your power really is enhanced perception."

"Yes."

"Okay. Okay. You're not lying."

"What makes you say that?"

"Because that's lame and—" She stopped herself. "Shit, sorry."

"I am so used to it."

"You wouldn't say that drunk if you could stop time is my point," she almost ducked down to grab another drink but thought better of it. "So, that makes us..."

We'd reached this impasse several times in the last hours. I scanned her. The lines on her face. The size of her irises. She was worried. Apprehensive.

So I said it first.

"We're soulmates."

Emma's gaze shifted downward and to the left, considering instead of answering.

"Why else would one of us display a power we'd never seen before? Unless you're right and someone was stopping time for everyone but me and—"

"And the woman who's immune to powers," she cut in. "Maybe we are soulmates, but turn it off."

"It's not—"

"Toby, please."

"I don't—" I stopped short and instead tried even though I didn't know how. My perception was passive. I didn't get to choose whether I used it. Was there supposed to be a switch somewhere inside my head? Was I—

How long had it been at this point? Six, seven hours? We'd planned to meet pretty late and it would almost be light out by now. She was right. We had to get—

"I don't know how," I admitted, "if it's me."

Emma opened her mouth to say something, then reconsidered. Her perfectly manicured nails were digging into the vinyl of the bar top.

"Okay. It's been lovely, but if you getting here started this then," I said as I stood up, "maybe I just need to leave, and that will turn it off so we can figure out what's going on." I took the first steps toward the door.

"That's a good plan," she nodded along with what she was saying, like she was convincing herself, "I'll reach out to you. It was an excellent date."

"Let Todd know for me," I added as I reached the door; a second later, I stepped into the chilled early-fall air. The door didn't shut behind me, so I kept walking until I would have been out of eyesight.

Then I stopped.

Should I have turned around? What were the chances that she was my soul mate? What was I leaving behind if I didn't see her again? It was a dumb thought, but the idea of walking away started gnawing at me.

But what choice did I have? In front of me, a couple was frozen in the middle of a quiet conversation on the way to the bar. Soul mates only affected one another when they were close by. I took a few more steps and started to sprint.

I was three blocks away when the world stuttered around me. My vision blurred, and the moonlight was shattered by the sun. I stumbled, almost crashing into a woman dressed like she was on her way to brunch.

Shit. I'd left my jacket at the bar, but—

I checked my watch; 8:06 AM.

2

Zoe - Morning After

I took a deep breath and centered my attention on the heavy bag in front of me, pulling my power away from it and letting it swing back and forth on its chain. One more deep breath.

My power lashed out before my fist could, knocking the bag out of the way and reach. I growled and grabbed it with my mind, locking it back into place and holding it taut on the chain.

"Come on. You got this," I whispered. Self-talk always felt dumb, but it worked. Someone had to be in the room giving you positive feedback. Might as well be you.

I let the telekinetic hold on the heavy bag slip. Just one successful punch, and I could call it a day.

Deep breath.

It was my mind. My power. I was in control. It had to listen to me. I wanted to punch this thing with my fist, not just hit it. If I wanted to hit it, I would have been trying to use my power and—

"There you are."

Telekinetic power jabbed the heavy bag out of spite as I broke concentration. "I could say the same thing, Emma." I didn't need to turn to see who it was, considering she was the one person I couldn't feel walking into a room. That and I knew her voice. "Where were you?"

"It's complicated."

"Date went that well?" I grabbed the towel on the other side of the room and threw it to myself.

"It's complicated," she repeated. I frowned at that. I usually appreciated the fact that I couldn't read Emma, but sometimes, it made talking to her infuriating.

I heard Emma sit on the bench beside the door and pick up my water. She clicked the bottle closed.

"Is that all the information I'm getting?" I asked.

"How does being at the bar at 8 in the morning sound?"

"Makes me wonder what bar in this city is open that late." I wrapped my mind around the heavy bag to stop it swinging before turning around to look at her. "Last night's clothes?" I asked.

"Didn't really have time to go change. I was already running late."

"Because you were at the bar until 8?"

"Exactly."

I walked over to Emma, feeling my usual sphere of influence dampen with each step. By the time I'd sat beside her on the bench, I couldn't feel anything else in the room. For a blessed moment, I was blind. It was just me and her. "What's complicated about that?"

Emma held up the water, asking permission. I waved a hand to tell her to go ahead. "Can you look someone up for me?" she asked.

"Can't you?"

"I'd prefer not to be the one to do it," Emma answered before taking the sip she'd asked for.

"Name?"

"Toby Vander."

"Todd's friend?"

Emma nodded. Luckily, with her, I didn't need to explain how I knew things like that. I heard things, thoughts, as I walked by people. Most of the time, I could ignore the cacophony, but sometimes you picked things up.

I pulled out my phone to look him up in our system. "Just anything about him?"

Emma didn't respond, which I took as a yes.

"Am I looking him up for good reasons or bad reasons?"

"Fine reasons."

"So, bad reasons."

"Fine reasons," she repeated.

"Fine it is." I waited a second as my phone did its work, checking the database and letting me know whether he had a public file or if I was going digging in the archives. "What am I looking for here?"

"I need to know what his power is."

"You went home with him, and you don't know what his pow—"

"I didn't go home with him," she corrected. Emma was the one person who could lie to me, and she might have been, but she was still put-together for someone who'd had a wild night.

"So you..."

"Were at the bar until 8 in the morning. Stayed at the bar the whole time."

"And don't know what his power is," I added for her. I didn't look up from my phone, but I could feel the eye roll. His profile popped up on the screen. "Well, if this is the guy, then—" I scrolled down the file past the innocuous information like height and found what we were looking for. "Enhanced perception."

"That's it?"

"Yup." I offered her the phone. She didn't take it.

"So he's not in the DPD?"

"Why the fuck would enhanced perception be in the DPD?" I asked. I was in the dangerous powers database. Hell, Emma was in there, but she'd gone off the deep end if she thought knowing the difference between Oxford Blue and Royal Blue Dark was worth a paper file.

"I didn't think he was telling the truth," Emma explained, "because it doesn't add up."

"Why? Was he wearing dark navy instead of black?"

"I need you to take this seriously."

"I need you to be honest with me."

Emma took a deep breath and clasped her hands in her lap. "Look, it's complicated."

"Cut the shit. You know I'll just try to figure out what happened if you don't give me a straight answer, so—"

"Not here," she said.

"Pardon?"

"Not here."

I looked down at the stunningly average profile on the phone and then back to Emma. She was already standing.

"Zoe, I don't feel well, so I'm going to head out a little early— Um, just if anyone asks about me, I went home sick, okay?"

Now that. That wasn't like Emma. No, that set off alarm bells. "Okay."

"Thanks, Zoe. I'll talk to you soon."

I didn't answer as Emma slipped out of the gym and left me alone. Once she was far enough down the hallway, I could feel the room with my power again. My mind ran over each weight and machine, prodding at them, testing them. Meanwhile, I was still staring down at the profile on my phone.

What was so special about Toby Vander?

By the time Emma was gone, I understood I needed the answer to that question, but if Emma wasn't even willing to give me all the details, I couldn't exactly put out a search request for him.

No, if she wanted to know about Toby Vander, I'd need to go to the archives myself to ensure that there wasn't anything there on him. After all, according to his file, his power might have been innocuous, but it was Omega rarity. He was the only instance of the power that we knew about.

Honestly, considering the fact that most of my coworkers and our problems tended to have high-level versions of common powers, it was interesting to deal with something other than raw strength. Was he strong? Based on everything I'd seen, no. Toby Vander was a mystery.

Well, he himself wasn't much of a mystery, but it was about what would make Emma so cagey.

The archives were three floors down from the gym, well into the basement of the head office. Most people hated the damned place, but it was sometimes almost cathartic to go through our old paper logs, every note and comment that we couldn't risk a technopath getting their hands on. Others complained classic paper and ink were heavy, but that had never been an issue for me.

But then again, I always took the stairs because I disagreed with elevators. Everything was a trade-off when you climbed high enough on the power scale.

There was always someone in front of the archives, a token guard who paid attention to who was signing in and out of the place. After all, it was room after room and box after box stuffed with sensitive information. Today, the man on duty was Rod. All I'd need to do was—

My phone buzzed in my pocket.

Hey, I know what you're going to do. Please don't.

It was Emma.

I stopped in the stairwell, leaning against the railing and letting my power float the phone in front of me. I almost hated the fact that Emma was right. The whole point of coming down here had been to investigate for her, but now she'd asked me not to.

I frowned at the message.

Or at least she'd implied I should do it through something other than official channels.

I took a deep breath. Who needed the archives anyway? As long as Toby Vander was in Crescent, I could find him.

Tracking someone telepathically was like casting a net. I pushed my power out, and it would snag on their brain as long as I was asking the right questions. Having a name made it easy, and knowing what he looked like made it child's play.

Even then, I took a second deep breath before closing my eyes to open up my perception because the moment I did, the waking world gave way to the pounding heartbeat of a million thoughts competing for my attention. Flared emotions brushed past me as I combed over the city.

I can't believe Collin called in again today.
What the hell was Thomas thinking?
He can't know.
How are we going to afford this?
I—

I pulled hard on a thread of thought, anchoring myself on it and honing in. Sweat dripped down my forehead. I wouldn't have to push far into their head to grab a phone number. I could have gotten more, but that was about as much as I wanted to prod around at this range.

A second later, I snapped my eyes back open as the stairwell door did. I dropped to the ground out of habit. I hadn't even realized I was floating during my search.

"Oh, it's you," Todd said from the bottom of the stairs. He was a big man, usually only called to the archives during serious shuffling. He was doing someone a favor if he was here on a Sunday.

"What's up, Todd?"

"Didn't know what was going on. Door was rattling, but…" Todd shrugged instead of explaining the rest. That was just how things worked around me. "Were you coming down to the archives?"

"Thought I needed to look someone up, but I figured it out."

"Oh." He pulled back a little from the door. "Okay. Well, let me know if you need anything." He went to return to whatever he was doing, but I held the door in place with my power. Of everyone in the office, Todd had the best chance of closing it despite me, but neither of us wanted to test the door.

"You brought Emma out last night, right?" I asked. "Close friend. Blind date."

"Yeah, that was last night."

"How'd that go?"

"You didn't ask Emma?" That was fair. Emma and I were practically sisters and were neighbors.

"Didn't see her last night."

Todd opened his mouth to say something. Based on his surface thoughts, it was more about his friend than Emma.

"So?" I asked.

"Don't wanna go into detail because...Well, not my place. But they really hit it off. Got that energy, you know?"

I waited for him to continue, but he didn't. "That's all the information I'm getting?"

"That's everything I'm saying." Fair point. I could have dove into Todd's memories if I'd wanted, but at least Todd told me that Emma hadn't been in danger last night.

"I can respect that." I let go of the door, and it jerked a little in his hand. "Glad it went well."

"I really think so. I told her he was a good guy. It took a bit of convincing to get her out, but, man, I think it's a good match, and I have a head for that sort of thing."

"Didn't think she'd be into the blind date idea."

"She wasn't. Think she's glad she did it now, though."

"Good to hear." I took my first steps back up the stairs.

"Hey, Zoe. Since you're down here, would you mind helping me move a couple of things? Zach's got me in on a Sunday and—"

"I have a couple calls to make, but I'll be back after lunch to help if you still need it."

"Thanks, Zoe," Todd said, but I heard him thinking he'd be finished by lunch.

That was too bad. Todd was a nice guy, but I had something more pressing to deal with: Toby Vander.

3
Toby - Found

I almost wasn't sure how I'd gotten home. After leaving the bar, everything had fallen into a blanket of white noise. What was supposed to be a bus ride had turned into a crisp walk through the fall morning. I had hoped that staring at the sidewalk would help me think, but it didn't.

No, I'd gotten back from my date just after nine and hadn't let things settle in until I'd taken a warm shower to make up for forgetting my jacket. The hot water steamed up the small bathroom, and I watched as the mirror fogged over, blurring my reflection into obscurity.

I didn't know what to make of it.

Soulmates.

Stopping time?

It had been a fucking blind date. Those were supposed to be disasters and a funny story if I was lucky. Instead, it was life-changing. If all of that was real, then...

Could I stop time? What did that even mean? How could that even work?

Questions like that kicked off my descent into a rabbit hole about the rules and limitations of powers. There were levels of understanding about it, from learning the Omega scales in school to watching interviews with experts to documentaries on Patient Zero.

Now, I was taking a step beyond all of those and wading knee-deep through doctoral dissertations.

It was understood until 1984 that abilities required a matter-energy anchor point to function…

Though such abilities are theoretically possible, the caloric requirements render them unsustainable…

Controlled testing repeatably proves that abilities which reportedly break these tenets simply achieve similar effects with methods that…

Blood samples prove a reliable method for understanding difficult-to-categorize abilities and…

Introducing a bonded pair can adjust the abilities of one or both members. The greatest effects occur when the subjects are within…

Once my head was spinning from scientific language and attempting to decode the difference between theoretical and proven, I tried looking up my situation.

Conspiracy theories. No matter how I reworded the question, I only found people convinced they had some impossible power with elaborate excuses as to why they couldn't use it or prove it.

Maybe I was one of those people. After all, I was trying to understand if I could stop fucking time. From what I understood of the research papers, that was impossible.

All of this was supposed to be impossible.

Supposed to be.

I kept my following searches vague to avoid the conspiracy rabbit hole articles about power regulation. Criticism of government methods. Extremist protests over the past year. Callum Rehsman.

I bit my lip and took a deep breath before I switched tactics.

Emma Tavish.

First thing. She was practically a ghost. I'd figured anyone in the DPR would be on the front page every second day, but that wasn't the case. She showed up in occasional articles as a vessel for quotes but was never the star of the show.

Then there was her government-mandated profile. Everyone who worked in the public sector had one, but hers...

Hers was the longest I'd seen by far.

Exudes a mental wave in the surrounding air that disables and prevents the use of others' abilities. The effects begin at 34092 cm from the subject and become more drastic as the subject approaches.

I skipped down the page. Her file contained an incredible amount of detail, and she hadn't been kidding about it being wordy.

The nature of the subject's power has them under watch as a potential—

My phone rang back on the kitchenette counter and I jumped, closing Emma's profile as I did. I lived alone, but leaving her information on the desktop felt wrong.

Maybe I shouldn't have been looking her up in the first place.

I grabbed the phone and took a second to wipe off the screen before answering. "Todd."

"Bout time you answered."

"My phone hasn't rung since I got home."

Todd paused on the other side, and I took a deep breath. He didn't have context, which meant that—

"So, you didn't go home last night." I heard the stupid grin in his stupid voice.

"I never said that."

"You don't miss phone calls."

"Like I said, you didn't call me this morning."

"No, I called you last night. Tried to get an update once I got Soo to bed, but you didn't pick up."

That made sense. Emma and I'd never left the bar. The baffling part was that Todd was speaking like I'd been there at all, even though I couldn't have spoken to him after Emma arrived and—

When I'd snapped back to reality, it had been the middle of the morning. Time must have passed. Todd must have seen something when he was frozen.

"I know you're trying to come up with an excuse right now," Todd said, interrupting my thoughts. "I can give you a few more seconds if you need 'em."

"I'm not."

"Bullshit."

"I'm just thinking, Todd."

"About an excuse."

With nothing else to say, I relied on a classic. "Fuck off."

He sighed. "Look, I'm not fishing for details. At least not too many. I just wanna know thumbs up or thumbs down. Seemed like you two were really getting along. Got along? Whatever."

"We did." At least I could be honest about that part.

I tucked the phone between my cheek and shoulder and made my way back to my computer. I went to continue my searches but came up blank.

"You really don't want to talk about it, huh?"

"Sorry. Just off in space. It went well."

"That's it?"

"What do you want from me?"

"More than 'It went well.' I thought I was being a bro by ducking out early."

"You also needed to get Soo home."

"That aside."

I nodded to myself about getting that one right. It wasn't hard to figure out what happened with context clues. Soo-jung was a sleepy drunk, and Todd over-served. "The night finished up...okay?" The pause wasn't intentional, but it was there.

"Just okay?"

"Well, I—"

"Did you blow it at the end? Seriously? That date wasn't going 'Just okay.'"

I was about to snip back at him, but I had to figure out my cover. I didn't know about the date Todd saw, so I had to—

My phone vibrated against my cheek. Unknown number.

Emma?

"Todd, I'll call you back."

"Is it, Emma?"

"Todd."

"Fine. Fine. Call me back."

I answered the new call without taking the time to say goodbye. "Hello?"

There was a pause on the other end, followed by practiced speech. "Toby Vander. This is Zoe McCourtney from the Department of Power Regulation—"

I hung up the phone before I thought about what that meant. The DPR was serious. They were the people in charge of—It was also where Emma worked.

Shit.

The phone rang again. I picked it up.

"I'm going to suggest you don't do that again," she said on the other side.

"This is Toby Vander. Yes. Sorry."

"Toby. I'm Zoe McCourtney. Field Suppression Agent for the Department of Power Regulation. It's nice to meet you."

"Nice to meet you, too."

"I have a couple of questions for you."

"Is this about Emma?"

She paused. "Toby, this is a personal line, but let me finish. I would like to ask you some sensitive questions. Meet in person."

I opened my mouth to speak, and it was almost like she sensed it.

"No need to discuss the subject over the phone. As I mentioned, this is a personal line, but I think this should be a face-to-face conversation."

I understood the context there. Ms. McCourtney didn't want to say anything on a potentially recorded call.

"Does that sound good to you?" she asked.

"Okay." I looked up her name. It rang a bell, but nothing as prominent as Callum's.

"There's a lovely sandwich place on Harrington. Close to the DPR office just down from the North Bridge."

"Are we meeting there?" I asked. I brought up the search results. I'd never understood the expression of blood running cold until then.

"For both of our sakes, Mr. Vander, please stop looking me up."

I froze at that comment.

"Whether or not that was a lucky guess is something I can answer at lunch. No more searches about me, or the Department... Or your situation. Am I making myself clear?"

I took a deep breath. You heard stories about people at the top of the power scale—the same things that had made me hang up the phone when she mentioned the DPR, but feeling them first hand?

That was different.

I closed the browser I'd been using to search for Zoe and turned the computer off for good measure.

I'd been thinking for too long.

"Is that clear, Mr. Vander?"

"What's the name of the place?" I got up paced around the room as I asked.

"No need to put that in writing. You'll find it," she said. "I'll be outside. If you miss it, I'll stop you."

I opened my mouth to say goodbye, but it was dry, and I found a question instead. "Should I be nervous about this?"

"We'll figure that out."

"What's that supposed to mean?"

"It means that I'm working on it. Memorize this number in case you need to reach me. I know you can. Don't add me as a contact. See you at 11:30."

I took another deep breath, half to accept my potential fate and half to accept that I was pulling an all-nighter. "11:30."

"Perfect." She ended the call, and I fell down into the well-loved chair I kept in the corner for guests. I hadn't been holding my breath, but my lungs burned like I had.

The most powerful telepath on the continent wanted to know about last night. Meanwhile, I was still trying to understand what'd happened myself.

I stared at my reflection in my phone. At the massive bags under my eyes. I could ask Todd about Zoe. He might know her. Maybe he could reassure me about everything that was going on. Did asking Todd for Emma's number count as reaching out to someone about this? Was Zoe going to grab my phone at the meeting and check all of my messages? I could probably just ask him and—

No, Zoe had told me to keep this quiet, and I wasn't about to test her patience. I wasn't sure how much she had.

Todd wouldn't be happy about getting his call back blown off via text, but we'd done worse to one another a thousand times before. Right now, I had to get ready and figure out how I was going to get on Zoe's good side.

I didn't have a choice about whether I went to the meeting, but if I lied to myself enough, I could change how I felt about it.

Then again, there was a reason the DPR was in the news so often.

4

Toby - Lunch Meeting

There was a strange air on the waterfront for a Sunday afternoon, but I was probably the one carrying it. While everyone else here was working or taking a lovely walk, I was constantly considering going home. Not that it would do me any good. Zoe would find me at home as easily as she had found my number. At least, if everything I'd heard about powerful telepaths was true.

Just before I got to the place I figured Zoe had described on the phone, I took a distracted step a little too far to the right of the sidewalk, and a passing speedster almost flattened me. They swore at me. I swore at the city for adding more speeder lanes in the core.

DiRezzo's was a sandwich shop that matched Zoe's description. A place I'd noticed before but never wandered into. Outdated drapery hung in the front windows, and between them, a sign told me to wait to be seated. I'd always figured if I was getting a sandwich, I should be able to walk in, get my sandwich and leave. No menu needed.

To the right of the door was a young woman who couldn't have been taller than 5'3 on her tiptoes. She hid fire-red hair under the gray hood of a well-worn jean jacket and had a cigarette tucked between her teeth. Streaming smoke clouded her mirrored glasses.

As I ran my eyes over her, she perked up and caught my gaze. I hadn't said anything. By all accounts, I should have blended into the crowd. Should have. Could have. Didn't. She nodded and went back to staring at the sidewalk. I approached.

"Toby," she said without bothering to look up. That was telepaths for you.

"Zoe."

"Glad you could make it." Zoe peeled herself off of the wall and held out a hand. As she did, her glasses jumped off of her face and tucked themselves in her breast pocket. I accepted the handshake. "No trouble finding the place?" she asked as she turned. Before she could walk into the 'Please Wait to Be Seated' sign, it politely scooted to the side and then replaced itself as I followed her.

"I figured it out," I said. We had strode past the sign telling us to wait, and there were waitstaff in earshot, but if they cared, they weren't showing it. Zoe took a sharp left and led me up a red-carpeted staircase with the walls on either side plastered in framed photos of celebrities that had eaten here. I counted the faces on the wall. Anything to fill my mind instead of giving her something to read.

Not that I could stop her. I knew enough to understand that, if she really wanted to get something, she'd find it. That said, I figured idle thoughts would be the ones to get me in the most trouble.

Zoe reached the top of the stairs and took another confident left, walking past three more doors. This place clearly used to be a house, but I'd been in Crescent for twenty years, and I'd never seen anything other than a restaurant here. I would have guessed they'd use the tangle of rooms upstairs for storage, but there was a reserved sign at the end of the hallway.

It, like the sign downstairs, got out of Zoe's way. Everything did.

There was a small table in the middle of the used-to-be bedroom. The worn legs told me it had been there for a long time, and the only new thing in the space was the tablecloth and maybe the already-filled glasses of water on the table if we were lucky. Zoe got out of my way at the door, and the chair to the right pulled away from the table.

"Sit."

I complied as one menu threw itself at me, but I caught it before it made contact. Zoe sat down across from me. As she settled in, her hood pulled back, and her jacket straightened out, losing any wrinkles it had gained during the walk.

Zoe didn't pick up a menu.

I waited for a moment for a prompt from Zoe, then, without one, opened the menu. I'd made the right call avoiding this place. Who the hell would pay that much for a sandwich?

"It's worth the upcharge."

"What?"

"Quality's worth the price," Zoe said. "When you have to eat as much as I do, it's nice to treat yourself every once in a while." Her water rose from the table. "Plus, I'm paying, so you don't need to worry about it."

"That's generous."

"Well, I invited you out."

That didn't mean that—

"I know you can cover yourself, Toby. It's an offer." She cut me off at the thought. I was used to being a step ahead in a conversation by 'reading' body language. She took it to a whole other level.

A blonde waitress poked her head into the room. Zoe stepped in before she spoke. "The usual, Karen."

"I'll do that too," I added. The waitress turned heel out of the room, taking several quick steps down the hallway to put some distance between herself and Zoe. I felt my menu tug itself out of my hands, and then it flitted across the table to fold on top of Zoe's. The telepath turned her piercing blue gaze to me.

"Thanks," she said, "I like my eyes too."

"Are you going to stay in my head?"

"I can't not be there. I hear surface thoughts from everyone close. I couldn't ignore you if I wanted to, Toby."

That was unsettling. "Interesting."

Zoe shrugged. "Unsettling or not, it's who I am." She was having a conversation with my thoughts instead of my mouth. "Just say what you're thinking. It'll make this easier."

"Why are we at lunch?" I asked.

"Emma asked me to look into you."

"The Department of Power Regulation?"

"We both work there, but this isn't a work conversation."

Did that mean that she wasn't a—

"I am a Field Suppression Agent of the Department of Power Regulation. I am not here as one."

"Why tell me you were one on the phone?"

She leaned in. "It got you here. The title is usually convincing."

Zoe let the silence hang for a moment, and my glass of water scooted an inch toward me. I circled back to the first and maybe more important part of this. "Emma asked you?"

"Mhm."

"About what?"

"So," she dragged out the word like a curious mother, "what happened last night?"

"Do I need to answer?"

"Yes."

"Why? You're just going to read it out of me, and I'd prefer not to."

"Because people have conversations, Toby." Zoe brushed her hair out of her eyes; it fell back down to where it had been. "This is more about you playing along than it is about me discovering anything. You're right. I could force the story out of you, and you'd barely notice it was happening, but... I think that would get us off on the wrong foot."

"Is this the right foot?"

"It's better than a lot of other options."

I took a deep breath and then a sip of water. The wallpaper in this room had been replaced recently, but they'd tried to keep it in the same style as the rest of the house. "Nothing happened last night," I lied.

"You're funny. How'd the date go?" Hiding anything seemed like a losing battle.

"Fine," I said, "at least I think so." With everything that had happened, I'd barely had time to untangle the whole thing myself.

"Better than fine, from what I've heard."

"From Emma?" I heard my voice perk up as I said it.

"Todd mostly. Emma's reaction this morning is why I'm here."

"What'd she say?"

"That's between me and her, Toby." She'd paused for a moment before answering, maybe considering telling me before thinking better of it.

"You get to keep secrets, and I don't? Doesn't seem very fair."

"Conversations with me never are." She finally let the water that she'd been holding in the air offer itself for a sip. "But you're reading my body language. Or trying to. Is that fair? What did you think about my pause earlier?" She smiled at the end. I couldn't know if she was enjoying my narration, but she was keenly aware of it.

There wasn't a point in keeping things from her, and I wanted to be on her good side. "Emma and I are soulmates."

Zoe cocked her head at that and squinted for a moment. I felt a pull somewhere deep behind my eyes, and then she broke into a smile. "Congratulations."

I took a second to reorient myself after she went digging.

"Soulmates, that's incredible." She was beaming as she spoke. The kind of genuine smile you saw at weddings. "Congratulations again. Color me jealous."

I opened my mouth to speak but quieted as I heard footsteps at the end of the hallway. The waitress came back into the room with a small plate carrying a single lemon slice. Before she could put it down, the slice jumped off and threw itself into Zoe's water.

The waitress didn't wait for a thank you before leaving. Zoe shut the door behind her.

"So, Todd brought you on a blind date last night."

"Well, I didn't go out on a date with Todd. Todd brought me to meet Emma." Zoe glared at me as I finished. I didn't know if it wasn't the time for jokes or if I'd botched the delivery.

"As far as I'd heard until now, things went well. You hit it off. Emma wasn't as put together as normal this morning."

I raised an eyebrow at that part; we were soulmates. If she'd seen Emma this morning, how did she not know that we were?

"See, that's the part I don't get," she said. It took me a moment to catch up with her commenting on my thoughts again. "If you and Emma are soulmates, why didn't she tell me?"

"What?"

"She's not the secrets type," Zoe sighed, "never tell her anything you don't want on a public database."

"Secrets?" I asked.

"She told me to look you up. She never said why."

"Why not?"

"That question's the reason I'm paying for lunch." She finally leaned back in the chair a little, a blessed moment of casual body language from her. "I saw Emma at the office. She didn't want to talk about it there."

"Okay."

"Which makes me think she didn't want any of our bosses to know what happened. Which isn't like her."

I nodded instead of saying okay again.

"Emma's a touchy subject with upper management. So I think she's worried about how they'll react to the next step."

"Pardon?"

"What happened last night with her power?" She asked. "I know I've been back and forth about my position, but for her, I'm sister first, DPR agent second."

Her tone and the general biology of the matter told me she meant sister as an expression of close friendship. That said, how open could I be about last night? Was I supposed to just admit it? Emma'd been freaked out, which meant—

Of course, before I thought it, she spoke up.

"I'll find out either way, Toby. Let's be on the same side. What did Emma do at the bar?"

"Emma?" I asked.

"Why wouldn't it be Emma?"

I let the comment hang for a moment. There was nothing else on my surface thoughts, so Zoe's eyes went wide after a second.

"Yeah," I said.

Silence took over. Zoe's jacket pockets buttoned and unbuttoned themselves several times. Then she swore. Once. Twice. Thrice.

"I feel like that's bad," I said.

"It's—" she took a second, "not great." Her fork started fighting with her knife as she tapped her fingernails on the table. "I was so sure that she would be the problem if this happened."

"Can I ask what the problem is?"

"You haven't taken the time to think about it. Have you?"

"I've been busy."

"That wasn't an accusation, Toby." She took a deep breath, and her buttons calmed alongside the cutlery. "Emma would have been thinking about it right away."

"Shit. About what it can do?"

"About what you can do." She corrected, emphasizing 'you' and, for the first time since I'd left the bar, the idea hit me as something other than an abstract concept.

Stopping time? The question was less about what Emma and I could do and more about what we couldn't do.

Zoe nodded alongside my thoughts. "Standard protocol would be to detain you and separate you from Emma until we determine what's going on."

She didn't meet my eyes as she said that. Lie. Or at least not the whole truth.

She glared at my thoughts and then continued. "Power Regulation isn't always pretty, Toby."

"Shit." Emma was my soulmate. There were 5 billion people on the planet and she was the one person I was supposed to be with. I had barely gotten the chance to meet her and now I was supposed to just give it up?

"I'm not doing anything," Zoe reassured, "yet."

"Yet?"

"Yet."

"Shit." It was repetitive, but it bore repeating.

"Realistically, I have to look into your power now that I know about it. I can't just ignore it."

"But," I added for her.

"But I can delay that process as much as I can and keep it on the —" she shrugged, "on the down-low, I guess. Off the record."

"How long can you delay?"

"That depends on a lot of things. Don't wanna make promises I can't keep."

"What decides what happens to me and Emma?"

"How much do you know about official power scales?"

By power scales, she meant the rating attached to people's powers. Greek alphabet letters assigned to both power and rarity as a quick classification system.

"That's the gist of it," Zoe said. "To most people, it's a fun game. You stop thinking about it once you're out of college, but to people like me." She pointed to herself as a representative of the Department of Power Regulation. "For us, we use the official scales to keep track of people and reference how dangerous they would be in a rogue scenario."

"You seriously use the elementary school system?"

"It's never been a measure of firepower. It's a measure of danger. How much public disruption could someone cause if they wanted?"

"Okay."

"First rating, rarity, tells us how much we know about your power. Part two is the disruptive potential to government function, but most people misconstrue that as 'strength.' You run a combined rating through our system, and it tells us if we need to keep a close eye on you."

"Okay."

"I'm a Sigma Psi," she said.

Holy shit. Zoe was a Psi? That was the level of power you saw in movies and read about in fantasy.

"Yeah, I know," she commented on my thoughts. "Kinda rare and cataclysmic. In my case, once I was ten, they put me under careful watch, sent me to specific schooling and I didn't have many career options."

That sounded unpleasant.

"I'm not complaining. This is the only job where I could ever take my powers for a walk, but..." she took a deep breath, this time grabbing the water with her hands to take a drink. "It's context, Toby. Just how it is. It's—"

"An unfortunate reality?"

"Life's unfortunate, Toby, but we deal with it."

I nodded along. She could read how I felt about that either way.

"You, in our database, are an Omega Beta. You are the only known instance of your ability, and you had no effective way of using your power to threaten the DPR. Thus, little study, and near zero oversight."

"Until now?"

"I'm getting there. Emma was and is an Omega Tau. Less than three people have ever had her power, and she could be a walking disaster if she wanted to be. If it weren't for her limited range, she'd have a higher ranking." Zoe put the water back down and checked the door to ensure the waitress wasn't coming in. "Even with her range, she was under surveillance watch until she joined the DPR. Didn't have to do the school shit that I did, though."

"And what ranking do you think I have now?"

"That's what we need to figure out before someone catches onto us." I could tell the inclusive language was intentional. At least she wanted us to be on the same team. "If we don't figure it out first and they catch on, they'll—"

"Arrest and separate," I finished for her.

"Yeah. Sure. That."

"You don't know what we are based on what you saw up here?" I pointed at my hair.

"I went through your head, Toby, and you don't understand what's going on. I only have your perception to go off of right now, so—" Zoe ended the thought early as the waitress opened the door with a pair of sandwiches. If the bread and presentation were anything to go off of, they were worth the money.

Once the waitress had scooted out, Zoe closed the door and continued.

"So, right now, neither of us knows what's going on. The first thing we need to do is figure out whether you can actually stop fucking time."

"What if I can?" I asked.

"That's the worst-case scenario."

"I want to know." I took a deep breath to prepare. You read enough news over a lifetime to understand that crossing the government wasn't smart. Everyone described power regulation as a 'compromise'. One Zoe'd just admitted wasn't always pretty.

"Time stopping would be reality warping." She took a second to consider her delivery. "We don't understand the broader effects of a power like that."

"Okay."

Zoe watched the door for a second, but I could tell it was an excuse, giving her time to find the words. "I couldn't leave you with Emma if you kept using your power. Probably couldn't let you stay either way."

"I don't know how to turn it off."

"Even worse," Zoe got out before she swore under her breath. "Being positive. It's likely your power is just a weird isolation class effect." She said the words, but I didn't need to read minds to understand she didn't believe them. "If that's the case, then everything's fine, and this is all just a scare. I'll be at the wedding and throw in a nice gift for the trouble."

"Sounds great," I offered. She wouldn't have to read my mind to understand I was forcing it.

"Toby."

"Mhm?"

"This is new to you, but I need you to understand that nobody learns about this," she said. "If anyone finds out, it's a shit show."

"Okay."

"You need to stay quiet. Nobody else in the DPR will be this nice if they find out what you can do. Hell, that's if you're lucky."

"Lucky?"

"Lucky enough that the DPR finds you first."

I stared at the table but, at the same time, looked right past it. How was I supposed to do that? Did Todd know anything? How could he know anything? "How would I keep a telepath from learning?" I asked.

"They won't be looking, so you should be fine. As for the other questions, that's what we need to figure out. Okay?"

I nodded along. I didn't know who I could go to about this, but I could at least work with her.

"Don't mention any of this over the phone. Don't look up stuff online. Don't look for Emma. Don't..." she sighed and leaned back in her seat again. "I'm sorry. I'm not trying to freak you out."

"You're not," I lied.

"Keep your head down and act casual until I can find a place where you and Emma can be in the same room for some tests. I'll get you a burner phone so you won't have to use yours. Do whatever you'd normally do on a Sunday."

"Go home and sleep?" I suggested.

"That's..." Zoe cocked her head, and I saw the edges of a frown forming.

"I've been up since last night. Emma and I didn't get to sleep at the bar."

Zoe's frown, and the judgment that'd come with it, softened. "Then go do that. Just don't stand out. Act normal."

I nodded again. At least that part made things feel like a spy thriller as opposed to an imminent threat. "Thanks for helping me."

"I'm helping Emma," she clarified. "As long as you're what's going to make her happy, I'll stick my neck out for you. I'm on your side." Zoe took a deep breath and pushed her sandwich away. Must have lost her appetite. "And Toby?"

"Yeah?"

"If you are an Omega Omega, and if I have to do something." She took a second breath to steady herself. "I'll give you a head start."

5
Zoe - Debriefing

Emma and I'd lived together for years under Department Orders. I'd been an angry pre-teen, and she had both the personality and literal power to keep me from going nuclear. Three years ago, they gave me permission to move out and live on my own.

Now, Emma and I lived beside one another instead of together. We had a pair of condos at the end of a hallway where Emma's power wouldn't bother anyone but me.

And it wasn't a bother to me. When my reach faded away, it felt like coming home. The cacophony of Crescent's thoughts slid into the background as I approached the door. By the time I reached the small, fall decorated table she'd set up outside of her place for mail, it was finally quiet in my head.

That silence was also how I knew Emma was here. Which was good. I had questions.

A lot of them.

I idly ran one of my fingers across the dried red and yellow flowers on Emma's table. I didn't have a plan of attack, but that didn't matter.

Emma opened the door before I reached the handle. Luckily for her, I couldn't grab it from across the hall when she was around. Emma waited in the doorway for a moment, scanning me. She was still in last night's clothes, save for a new jacket, which meant she still hadn't slept. Of course, that was obvious even if she had changed. The dark circles under her eyes and tangled hair were all the evidence anyone needed.

"What did you do?" Emma asked once she finished looking me over.

"Nothing."

"Why lie?"

"I'm not."

"Cool." Emma went to close the door, but I got my hand in the way first. She stopped short of shutting it on my fingers.

"Now you're closing doors on me?"

"What'd you do?"

"I—" I sighed. First, that damned enhanced perception guy, and now this? What did a woman have to do in this city to have a comfortable, one-sided conversation? "Can I come in first?"

A pause. "Sure. Don't mind the mess. I've been trying to figure things out without going online, and it's... well, it's going."

"What are you trying to figure out?" I asked. Emma let me inside, but I stopped right in the doorway. I'd once seen Emma take apart her spice rack to dust each individual bottle, which made the mountain of scattered and ripped paper in the middle of her living room floor something worth pausing over.

"Don't play dumb," Emma said. "And I said don't mind the mess. You're minding the mess."

I waved a hand, and several sheets stacked themselves on the floor. I couldn't use my power much when Emma was around, but I was strong enough to not be completely useless. "Loving the new decorations."

"Just a pile of every dumb dissertation I saved over the years," she sighed. "Nothing that covers this... situation, of course. Figured there might be similar cases but—"

"But it's all hearsay and conspiracy theories?" I suggested.

Emma nodded, then moved to the kitchen. I'd always been jealous of how she'd managed to keep her corporate condo warm and inviting, with little herbs on the windowsill and enough art on the walls to be charming but cluttered.

I took a seat on the other side of her countertop bar, resting my chin on my palm. "Yeah, those theories are all white noise, and if I hadn't met Toby, I wouldn't believe it myself."

I expected a snappy reply, but there was just silence in the room. Emma was staring at me, somewhere between aghast and indignant. I let her think for a moment. Emma finally spoke up just as I was about to continue myself. "You went to go see him?"

"I invited him out," I corrected. "It's different."

"Zoe. Really?"

"You weren't giving me any details, so I had to—"

"Yeah. I wasn't saying anything because this is a complicated fucking issue," she snapped.

I accepted it. Emma took a moment to compose herself.

"Sorry, just..." Emma restarted.

"Just it's a complicated fucking issue?"

"Yeah. That." She took a deep breath, pushed her hair back behind her ears, and corrected it. Once she'd gone through that cycle twice, she started pacing instead of fidgeting. The soft padding of her socks kept time in the room before she continued. "Did you figure anything out?"

"That you didn't tell me you'd met your soulmate."

"Zoe." She hadn't said sorry, but her tone did.

"It's important, Emma. Like, you're kidding me, right? That's a one-in-two-billion chance."

"Zoe, you know there's more to it than that. We need to think about this and—"

"Em."

"You're right," she said. "It just doesn't matter if I met Toby, if we can't ever be together, does it? I get to know they're out there, but, well, I already knew that. Everyone does."

"What do you mean, never?"

"You know what I mean."

"No, I don't," I corrected. It wasn't the whole truth. I knew what

Emma was implying. She was saying that the rules wouldn't let them see one another again, but that was a defeatist attitude I wasn't used to seeing in her. "We are less than a day into figuring this out. Once we've done that, we can celebrate..." I gave it a moment to sink in, but it didn't. I leaned across the counter to emphasize my point. "Like we should be."

Emma sighed.

"I'll look into this. I'll take him far away and ensure we don't run into each other while I figure out what's happening. Okay?" I asked.

"Callum—"

"Rehsman can wait. Once I've figured out how he works, we," I took time to emphasize 'we,' "can make a presentation about it. I can be very convincing."

"There's still a chance it's all bad news, isn't there?"

"Of course. There's always a chance. Toby might be some weird aberration that can bend reality that we have no chance of understanding or controlling. Literal end-of-the-world stuff." I smiled at the end to show that it was a joke.

Emma wasn't looking, and she certainly wasn't smiling.

"But it's way more likely that nothing weird is happening, and what you experienced with him is a minor localized effect."

Emma put her hands in the pockets of the jacket. It was too big for her, and it wasn't new. Toby's maybe, but it wasn't the time to ask either way. "End-of-the-world stuff. Right," she said once the pause had hung on too long.

"I didn't mean it, Em. It's all gonna be fine."

"How do we talk to him about it?"

"I don't think we do."

"What about everything else?" Emma said. "About what we do? About what's going on?"

I puffed out my cheeks and blew air at the last part. There were times around Emma when I wished I had my powers just so I could play with an object in the room as a distraction. Most of the time it was to avoid a question because questions like that were poisonous traps if I'd ever seen one.

I opened my mouth, but I didn't end up saying anything. Toby had to know about what we did, right? Everyone understood that Field Agents weren't pretty, and he'd been appropriately thrown while speaking to me, but... How much did he know? Emma'd been thinking about it. Even if Toby didn't stop time, even if it was just a localized effect that seemed to...

What could his power do? What would people do to get him on their side? Once you reached the deep end, powers stopped being fun facts and became matters of life and death.

Especially with the recent rise in—

"Yeah, the silence about sums it up," Emma said.

"It's fine. Toby doesn't need to know yet."

"Yeah. It's fine until someone figures something out, and he's not ready for—"

"Emma, I'm right here, and I know. I can keep tabs on him all day if you want me to." She didn't look convinced. "Look, he has two of the top people in the DPR on his side here." I stood up to join her in the kitchen, and she met me halfway. I almost offered a hug, but she'd kept her arms crossed. "Emma, we're undefeated. We can tell him all about it when we're ready. He's safe until then."

"When do we even do that?" Emma asked. "At what point? Do we wait until we know exactly what he does? Do we wait until we've told Callum? Do we wait until we haven't told Callum?"

"Okay, we're not, not telling Rehsman. We're waiting until we know more so that we can properly bring him up to speed."

"Yeah. Sure," Emma said. I frowned at that. If there was an agent with a rebellious streak in the office, and I didn't think there was, it certainly wasn't Emma.

No need to fight about it right now, though. "So, plan time?"

Emma's response wasn't instant, but it didn't have to be. "Plan time." She nodded. Emma pulled an elastic off her wrist to tie her hair back and walked me over to the pile of sheets she'd left scattered on the floor, which I'd half organized.

Once she'd led me over there, she started explaining the half-baked ideas she'd managed in her sleepless state. I listened and nodded along, but didn't agree.

I had a better idea, but Emma wouldn't like it.

6

Toby - Into Regulation

The Department of Power Regulation was nestled close to the middle of town, a brown building tucked between a dentist's and another dentist's office. I'd dropped Todd off there once when he'd been interviewing for his current position, back when I'd had a car, but I'd never had any reason to go inside.

Zoe explained it was one of the two hubs for the West Coast. There was an office here to look into cases like mine and keep tabs on those with Sigma-level powers or above. Zoe said she was the strongest person in the building, and I believed her. I couldn't imagine someone who could top the ability to pull an airplane out of the sky.

In addition to its threatening contents, the Department of Power Regulation felt unwelcoming, like it was there to watch the city rather than be part of it. If the architect had been trying to sour people's opinions of the department with his design, he'd done his job.

I was outside, just far enough away to avoid loitering allegations. Zoe had said 9:05, but I'd been here since 8:55, just in case. The street was Monday quiet, the kind of silence that you got from depression and the start of the workweek. Zoe told me she would 'take care' of my job today. I wasn't sure what she meant, but I figured I was fired.

The Department of Power Regulation was the second-largest

branch of the government. They monitored every birth, wedding, and, apparently, blind date in a bar to ensure nothing too dangerous for the general public popped up. Of course, dangerous was a broad term; Todd walked down the street with the power to chuck someone over a building. The key was that he, and most people, kept their hands in their pockets. If anything, the DPR was a bogeyman. A reminder that there were sharks in the water and you weren't as powerful as you thought.

They were a symbol. Not something you ever had to worry about.

Except for me.

Across the street, a young woman was half-attempting to canvas the few people that were still getting to work. She had one hand in the pocket of her black jacket and another holding out a clipboard to passersby. By the time I remembered not to stare, she'd caught my glance and was waiting for an opportunity to cross the street.

"Do you work there?" she asked once there was a break in the cars. She was pointing back to the department. Didn't know I exuded that aura.

I shook my head. "No, no, I'm meeting someone here."

"Why?"

"Meeting." It was an uncreative answer, but it was close to the truth.

"So you have a minute," she said with sudden cheer. This was what I got for talking to a canvasser, distracted. I hadn't even bothered trying for an excuse. "Do you want to sign?" She held the clipboard out to me, expectant.

"What would I be signing?" I asked as I took it.

"The Department of Power Regulation is in charge of regulating individuals born with Sigma-level powers or higher," she started. It was a practiced speech. "Some methods they employ are extreme, including prenatal blood testing to mark 'at risk,'" she said the last part in a skeptical tone, "individuals."

"Okay."

She held out the clipboard again.

"So, what would I be signing?"

"Oh, right. So this is a petition to inform the senate that we're against their current position to broaden that prenatal testing program. It's currently limited to, um,"—she looked down at her clipboard for reference— "limited to parents with 'high-risk' powers themselves. But they're looking to expand the program to cover most hospitals in the area and then worldwide."

"Right, because the genetic link for powers has been disproved, right?" I quoted one of the many papers I'd read last night at the girl. She lit up for a moment before souring once she realized I was giving the reason that the program was expanding, not agreeing with her.

"That's the reason they're giving, but it's infringing on—"

I turned around in the middle of her sentence as I felt a tap on my shoulder, but there wasn't anyone there. A second later, I heard the voice above me.

"Making friends?"

Zoe was about five feet above my head, floating in the air with her hair blowing in the breeze. She was wearing the same jean jacket as yesterday, but a uniform under it instead of casual clothing.

The girl across from me narrowed her eyes upon seeing the uniform, but didn't comment. Zoe cocked her head. "I got scanned, and I turned out fine," Zoe said as she let herself down on the sidewalk beside me. "I need him."

"I was just saying—" the girl started, but cut herself off as she realized Zoe had already turned her attention to me. It felt rude, but based on everything I'd read, these people must have been outside her workplace daily, so I understood where she was coming from.

"Sure, I'll sign. Why not?" I grabbed the clipboard away from her, adding my name to it before catching Zoe's glare. The girl got out of our way before Zoe spoke up.

"Really?"

"What's the harm?"

"What's the benefit?" Zoe countered. "You don't believe that shit, do you? They're just asking everyone to run around and do what they want." She shook her head.

If I were being honest with myself, I would never have given it that much thought. It was never a conversation that involved me. Hell, I hadn't even considered a hypothetical where it did.

"Oh fuck off, your life's been complicated for a day," Zoe sighed. "Just let them whine and get on with your day. It's healthier," she said. "If you give them signatures, they just keep coming back."

"Should we get a move on?" I suggested, instead of letting idle thoughts get me in trouble again.

"Let's. Come on." Zoe didn't bother waiting for me as she strode toward the building. The girl with the clipboard kept her eyes on us for a moment as we crossed the street and then let her attention get pulled by someone else walking by.

Before we were even on the right side of the street, Zoe raised a lazy hand, and the Department door opened inward. I didn't know if she unlocked it or powered through the lock. Either way, the door held in place until we were through, then slammed shut behind us.

The department's front hall was cold and sterile. The only color in the room was the globe-like insignia of the Continental Alliance emblazoned on the far wall in shining gold. On either side, there was a man and a woman, one holding lighting and the other carrying a barbell. The two most common powers: charge and burst.

Would they have to change the wall if speedsters surpassed burst users? Had they already designed that?

"Don't think we have a design. No." Zoe said before she walked across the room and rang the silver bell on a black marble front desk. There wasn't anyone there at the moment. Zoe waited for less than ten seconds before sighing. "Steve." She called out to the empty room.

The bell floated off the desk and rang itself half a dozen times.

As if on cue, a man scurried in from the left side of the room, shoving a creaking door out of his way. He shimmied in behind the desk. "Sorry, Zoe," he stammered as he got into his chair.

Zoe pulled back from the desk. Her hair flipped itself. "It's fine. Grabbing coffee?"

Based on how the man had barged into the room when she called his name, I'd expected her to be pissed at him for being late.

"Yeah. Went a little long, sorry. Issue with the damned pods again." He looked up at me. "Who's this?"

"Interview for a position. One of Emma's postings."

Well, that was one way to word it. I was certainly applying to be something to Emma.

Zoe shot me a glance at my thoughts, then turned back to Steve. "She told me I had to do the interview. Think he's a friend or something, and she just wants to give him the job." She shrugged at the end. I wasn't sure what the man's power was, but it wasn't enhanced perception. Zoe would not win any acting awards anytime soon.

"Why are you interviewing?"

"Ask her?" Zoe suggested. "She's always doing this kind of shit to me when I'm not on field duty."

Steve nodded along with the last point, and I noted it. I'd only had a few hours with Emma, and you could learn a lot about someone from their coworkers. "But an interview?" he asked.

"I don't know, man. I do what she tells me." Zoe flashed a smile, and the bell floated several inches off the desk again. "My day is already packed. Can I skip the papers and sign when I have time?"

"He needs to sign in."

"Really?"

"Really."

"Come on, Steve." The bell jumped down to Steve's paperwork from the top, customer-facing part of the desk. "Who's gonna get mad about the papers? Emma?"

"Yeah."

"She told me to bring him here," Zoe protested. "I'll take care of the paperwork if she asks."

Steve frowned and thumbed the stack of sign-in sheets on his desk. His gaze lingered on me for a second, and I did my best to stay expressionless and out of it.

"You and the fucking paperwork," Steve sighed as he looked down at his computer monitor. He tapped a couple of keys, and there was a buzz to our left. "Good to go."

"You're the best," Zoe added as she walked me over to the iron door that had just unlocked. She pushed me through and turned me right twice. There was little of note in the hallways; wall-to-wall cast-iron gray. The first break was a silver elevator door. Zoe pressed the button to call it down before we were within spitting distance.

Once we were in front of the elevator, it felt like the time for questions.

"Why not do the paperwork?" I asked.

"Well," she started, "for one thing, I hate doing it. That part wasn't a lie. Second, I don't want a paper trail saying you were here." She thought for a second. "Another reason why you shouldn't have signed that damned petition."

I rolled my eyes. "Fine. No paper trail. Why?"

"I'm not supposed to bring potential Omegas over for playdates," she explained. The elevator doors opened, and we stepped in. Zoe hummed to herself as we climbed.

Why was I here if I wasn't supposed to be in the building at all? Why was—

"To answer what you're thinking," she said, "I need some of the equipment in my office for blood work. Figured it would have been more suspicious to bring it all home with me so I could see you there."

"So am I a fugitive for breaking in here, then?" I asked.

"Only if you're actually an Omega, but then we have bigger problems, anyway."

"If I'm not?"

"Then the only rule you broke was skipping sign-in. You have friends in high places, so you'll be fine."

I wasn't sure if Zoe meant herself or—

"Well, I didn't mean Todd," she pointed out.

I took a deep breath. Having a conversation with Zoe around was exhausting. Having her reply to my thoughts was… certainly an experience.

"Then stop thinking so loud," she commented. I figured it was just to make a point. Once she'd gaged my reaction, Zoe finally clicked the seventh and eleventh floors as our destinations. The buttons for the thirteenth and eighth floors were missing. "Thirteen is superstition, and this elevator doesn't go to eight."

"Can you get out of my head for a few minutes?" I asked.

"It's my job to be in there."

"It's an invasion of privacy," I argued.

"First." Zoe's tone had changed from banter to annoyance with that comment. "You can complain to this department if you want, but it won't get you far. Second, you don't know what having a high-level power is like, Toby. I can't get out of your head. It doesn't matter whether I want to be there. As long as you're within twenty feet, I will hear every thought you have."

I let it hang for a second. "Sorry."

Zoe took a deep breath. The elevator jerked twice before jumping to motion. "You notice the stupidest things. Mind's so busy. Can you just think about normal things for a second?"

Was Zoe really wearing white at this time of year? It was almost November. She wasn't following any fashion rules I knew of.

"That's not how that rule works," Zoe answered.

Of course, it wasn't her fault. In the past years, the DPR uniform had added white in an attempt to improve the public image of its field agents. That backfired when the whites in the uniforms got bloody before reporters showed up.

"Point taken," Zoe said after a second. "Look. You notice things; I'm going to hear them. I'll try to chill on answering your thoughts if it bothers you."

"Thanks."

"At least for a while. It's normal for me, so if you're around for a long time, I expect you to get used to it."

"And you'll get used to how my attention works?" I asked.

"If I can," Zoe answered.

"Sounds like a deal," I said as I offered a hand to Zoe. She didn't look over. She didn't shake it. She said nothing. Why wasn't she...

I waved a hand in front of her face. Nothing. I'd stopped everything again. Now, I was a fugitive using my illegal power in a government building. That was the best way to solve your problems. Lean into them.

Then again, if I was doing this, Emma must have been nearby to trigger it. I wasn't 'emotionally charged,' or at least I didn't think I was. My soulmate had to be nearby to cause a power spike like this.

The issue was I was stuck in the elevator.

I took a deep breath and focused on... starting time? Unstopping time? Whatever it was called. I took deep breaths, but I was trying to break my focus on something I wasn't focusing on. There was nothing to release because I wasn't holding on.

Well then. The only thing that solved this last time was moving.

I pulled on the elevator door, edging it open inch by inch by yanking and shoving the thing. By the time I had it halfway open, I was dripping with sweat, and my forearms were screaming, but at least there was a way out.

Just had to be skinny enough to slip into the opening I'd made. Luckily, I'd either lost weight or overestimated how much space I needed because I wiggled myself onto the floor without any risk of getting stuck.

I dusted myself off after crawling on the floor and stared down the hallway in front of me. Like the one downstairs, it was nondescript, a page left intentionally blank.

Half a dozen doors were on either side of the hallway, but my eyes snapped to the one at the end, a gold nameplate, the only color in the hallway.

Emma Tavish: Head of Ability Research and Control

7
Toby - We Meet Again

I cracked open the door to Emma's office, and there she was, leaning back in her chair with her feet on the desk. "I was wondering when you would show up," she said. She tapped the spike of her high heel against the desk. "So this is you again?"

"I..." There wasn't a point in debating that was there? I didn't think it was me. She didn't think it was her, and none of this made any sense either way. "Seems like."

"Zoe brought you here?"

"Yes."

"I'm gonna kill her," Emma sighed. "Where is she now?"

"In the elevator."

"She should be fine there. Did it stop?"

"Stopped working."

"So that was her plan? Reach out to you and get you to come into the head office for testing..." Emma pinched the bridge of her nose before swinging her legs off the desk so she was properly seated. "This is such a mess."

"Did you not know about this?" I asked.

"She told me she was taking you far away to ensure this didn't happen again." Emma took a deep breath. She'd done her makeup differently today. It was safer, more corporate, less color. "But she's such a fucking cat."

"Pardon?"

"Curiosity's gonna kill her," Emma explained, "or I'll do it."

I left that for a second. Would it be better if I just left? No. Emma said the plan was to take me far away. I wasn't about to lose this chance for a proper conversation. "At least we found our soulmate. Right?"

"Yeah," she said like she agreed with me. Her voice had the tone of a child being forced to do chores. "Sorry," she said after a second, "I don't want to be negative about it, it's just that this,"—she motioned to the surrounding room—"makes this all so complicated."

"I..." I didn't want to say I understood because I didn't. Based on what I'd read about the DPR and what Emma did, there were layers to this I hadn't seen yet. "I empathize with that."

"And you should be the perfect soulmate for me," Emma continued in the same tone. "You're sweet, you're charming, your power is so innocuous that turning it off shouldn't matter...it's just —" She cut herself off with a half-groan.

"One more compliment and you'll have hit the rule of threes. Then I'll do you."

It wasn't much, but Emma snickered.

"Should I ask for an explanation of why this is so bad?" I started as I slipped into the chair across from her. "Or should I just leave it there?" The left leg of the chair was loose. That was going to get annoying.

"I don't love the fact that my soulmate falls under my job to terminate."

"Isolate?" I suggested.

Emma raised her eyebrows but didn't reassure me.

"We don't know if I stop time yet," I pointed out.

Emma motioned to the room around us. "You're technically right. There are other explanations. It's just..." She turned to her computer and jiggled the mouse. Then she hit a few keys on the keyboard before sighing. "Should have seen that coming," she mumbled to herself as she ducked to one of her drawers and pulled out a yellow notepad that said 'Don't Forget to Remember' in pink writing along the top.

"What else could it be?" I asked. "If I don't stop time."

"I don't know. Have you taken a blood test since you got here?"

"No."

"Why?" she asked.

"Because I stopped time."

"Or—" Emma cut herself off and rested her head in her hands, "something. There has to be a good answer here."

"Because?"

"Because I don't want my soulmate to be the reason that I go on the run from the government."

"Would there be another reason?"

Emma looked up at me and blew her hair away from her mouth. "I figured it would be Zoe who made me do it."

"Nice to know you had a plan."

"We did," she said. Emma looked down at the notepad and tapped the back end of her pen on it several times. "We were worried that they'd try to split us up. Just never happened."

"Sounds familiar."

More pen clicking. "I had more time to think about it with her. Didn't make the plan until I'd known her for years. Not... one day."

"Soulmates need to count for something in this case."

"That's fair." Emma sat up straighter and patted her hair down. It did little to correct the tangles she'd put into it. "So," she began as she turned the pen around, "do you think you can start time up again?" She scribbled on the notepad.

"No. Or at least I don't know how," I said. "I guess I can stop time. I don't know how to stop—" How could I even word that? "Stopping it."

Emma sighed. "You saw the door on the way in, didn't you?"

"Just your name."

"Enhanced perception." She rolled her eyes as she said it. "I'm Emma Tavish, Head of Ability Research," she said, sliding the notepad over to me. "This is what I have confirmed about us." The list was empty, save for two comments about the fact that time stopped and a line about us being soulmates circled three times.

"That's...progress?"

"Thanks." She grabbed the notepad back.

"You don't have anything else to add about your 'boring power?'" she asked. I could hear the air quotes.

"It is boring," I offered. Emma raised an eyebrow. "Was boring."

"Yeah. Was. Do you know how powers work?"

"Gonna assume that's rhetorical."

Emma nodded. "And I'll assume you remember everything from the second grade."

"So, what are you?" I asked.

"Pardon?"

"On the scale?"

"Oh." Emma went back into the drawer and pulled out an unopened pack of cigarettes. She set to opening it. "Omega Tau."

"Tau?" I asked, like I hadn't read her profile.

"I'm on the no-fly list. I can't be around chargers. People would die if I walked into a hospital..." She left it there, probably because she saw my eyes go wide. I'd been thinking of her powers in the way of turning off the flashy stuff some people could do, not how it could buckle utilities. "A lot of the city could get disabled if I was in the wrong place. So they gave me a government job, a pension, all that jazz, and in exchange, I get told where to stand."

"Pension sounds nice."

"Spousal as well, so that's great for us," she said. I could tell from the tone that she partially understood it as a deal with the devil, but at least it came with perks. "But then there's you."

"Me?"

"Yep."

"Figured out what I am on the scale?" I asked.

Emma tapped the empty notepad in response once she had the pack of cigarettes open.

"You smoke?" I asked after a second.

"These are actually Zoe's, but yes. Only when I'm stressed, though." I nodded along with that. At least she wasn't lying to herself by saying she was trying to quit. "Anyway, I know nothing about your power yet, but you're an Omega... something."

"Something? Last I checked, that isn't in the Greek alphabet."

There was a pause where she could have made a snide comment, but she let it pass. Instead, she looked me over. "Whatever you were, it's not the case anymore, which is pretty common when people meet their soulmates, but..."

"Zoe said Omega Omega."

"If you stop time."

I read her expression. "Which you don't think I do."

"I'm hoping you don't," she corrected, "and if you just stopped time, I wouldn't have been in the bar with a very confused janitor as soon as you walked outside." She tried the lighter, but it didn't light. "Was it the same for you?"

I nodded.

"So you didn't stop time; you skipped us through it," she said.

"Skip?"

"We don't have a term for everything in powers, but blinking is space, so skipping might as well be—"

"Time."

"Exactly. What happened to you once you were a few blocks away?" Emma asked.

"People were walking down the street, and it was 8:06," I said. "Nothing special, just like I was on my way to work with one hell of a hangover."

"So," she went to her computer and tapped the keyboard a few times, then stopped. "Right, right, right," she muttered before going back to the mostly empty notepad. "You break that."

"We break that."

"You stop time," Emma said.

"Not unless you're around," I countered.

"I already break people," she sighed. "You can break the

computer. Okay?"

I nodded.

"So. You were outside. I was inside. What did everyone else see?"

"Todd thought our date was going really well," I answered.

"That's it?"

"I didn't know how to talk to him about it without giving away that I didn't know what happened."

"So you didn't tell him?"

"No."

"Good." She wrote something down on the notepad. "So, that means Todd and Soo-jung have a different memory of the night than we do."

"I also think it was a good—"

Emma held up a finger to cut me off. I was going to tire of that real quick. Proof we were soulmates. "That means there were two versions of us at the time. A version that was there with Todd and then us..." Emma bit the end of the pen. "That's why Zoe fucking did this."

"What?"

"Zoe told me last night when we were planning that she'd talked to Todd. She knew he had memories you didn't. She wanted to test that, and she knew that I'd never agree to it."

"Okay. What are we testing here? What does this mean for our little notepad list?" I asked.

Emma was talking faster. There was excitement in her voice, passion. "In theory, only one version should control what happens in the 'real' timeline. If you can stop time for yourself—us—but can't affect anything or change the world, then we don't have a problem at all. The implications are astounding, but it wouldn't be dangerous and—"

"What if we affect what happens?"

"That"—Emma clicked the pen open and closed another half-dozen times—"That is a whole other can of worms." She put pen to paper and wrote as she mumbled to herself, "How would the drinks have even worked?"

"Okay. So, to help you do your job, I'll figure that out," I said. "What're the next steps?"

"You need to get blood work done." Emma stuck her pen in her mouth and spoke with it between her teeth. "Which means I need to go soon."

"Shame we have to end our lovely second date so soon," I said, laying the tone on thick so she understood it was a bit.

"I know, but if we wait too long, then Zoe might end up drawing the blood of the other version of you, and I'm not sure how that all works. The experiment takes precedence right now."

"It'll be nice once I'm not the experiment, and you can just come home and tell me about work."

"Ha," Emma said in place of laughing. "You can take the stairs at the other end of the hall, three floors up, and you're on the eleventh. Zoe's office is there."

I made a mental note that Emma was on the eighth. The secret floor. "Zoe's still in the elevator."

"The frozen her is," Emma said. "There is probably a version of you talking to her right now."

"Trippy."

"That's the shit I'm paid to deal with."

I stood up and smiled at Emma. She half-matched before looking down at the notepad and taking one last note. Once she had, she stood up.

My jacket was on the back of her chair. She grabbed it and offered it to me. "Here, you left it at the bar."

"You keep it," I said. "I'll grab it next time."

"There isn't supposed to be a next time for a while, Toby."

"It'll happen."

"It's cold today." She held out the jacket, insistent. I almost opened my mouth to say that I'd been fine in just a sweater on the way here, but why ruin the moment?

"Thanks," I said. "For grabbing it from the bar."

"Yeah," Emma sighed. She ran her hands through her hair again. "I should head out. You go upstairs, and Zoe will let me know when it's all clear."

"Sounds good." Should I have been reaching out to her? We were soulmates. Was I just saying goodbye by walking away again?

Emma was the only person on the planet who could be with me when I stopped time. We were meant to be together. We were going to fall in love. Was walking away now going to change that? Was—

"Toby?" she asked, just as I'd drifted off into thought.

"Yeah?"

"Stay safe."

Emma sealed it with a kiss, and for the first time since I'd gotten my powers, the world faded away.

I'd never felt something so powerful.

8

Toby - Bloody Work

When I reached Zoe's office, she wasn't there, which made sense, considering, as far as I understood, she was still stuck back in the elevator. Emma hadn't left the building yet, which gave me time to snoop.

If my math was correct, it also meant that we had to be further apart to break our little time bubble than we did to start it. It'd only kicked in on the elevator, but it was still here when I was further away.

I couldn't have explained what I expected heading into Zoe's office, but it hadn't been a bookshelf back wall filled with textbooks and essay collections. In the far left corner, hidden with the spines facing inward on the bottom shelf, there was a smattering of paperbacks that screamed romance.

Part of me wanted to check; the other part didn't want to snap into reality holding Zoe's secrets.

Outside of the bookshelf, there was a diploma on the wall from a university I didn't recognize and a desk covered in several dozen fidget toys. Based on what I'd seen at DiRezzo's, Zoe probably used them to keep her powers entertained while she was working.

I picked up a book in the dead center of the shelf, a smaller collection by a man named Dr. Zyke. I recognized the name. He had discovered the first symptoms of superpowers in the pandemic's aftermath. He was an oft-quoted man because there weren't many scientific sources documenting interaction between powered and unpowered people. That knowledge was a thing of the past. Hell, his stuff went back before people understood how soulmates worked.

I flipped open the book.

Subject Zero and I have spent the past several days speaking exclusively to one another. After some time working with him, I've found that he is just as frightened of his powers as I am, though his flames cannot burn him. Subject Zero seems apprehensive about his return to normal society, but admittedly, I am more concerned about whether there will be a society to return to at the end of our testing. Infection rates are only rising, and if those who survive unlock such astonishing abilities, I'm fearful as to how—

I shut the book. Middle school history, a primary source, but still middle school. Zoe might have had stuff here that I couldn't access at home. Did I need to be reading those? Would they help me out here? Would I...

At the top row of my reach, and just out of Zoe's, was a book with a false emerald dust jacket. I pulled it free, and dust showered down. I hadn't revealed a book as much as a pile of paper, barely contained by spiral backing.

Bingo.

I grabbed the slapdash book and flipped it over, blowing the dust away because dust jacket was just a fancy name. The front page had the title and author laid out in simple font.

Zoe McCourtney

A Look Into Fight or Flight Response in PSI Level Individuals.

A senior project.

I checked the first few pages, and confusion set in. Zoe's writing used industry terms freely, and I didn't have enough evidence within the first sentences to help me wrangle context from them. I flipped through further pages, searching for a conclusion, but I only got as far as the abstract.

The world lurched. I heard the office door open and close several times behind me. Then there was quiet.

"Enjoying yourself?" It was Zoe who was now in the office with me… or had she always been there? Hard to say. The thesis pulled itself from my hands and jumped back into its slot on the bookshelf. The dust jacket followed.

"I feel like I should try to understand some of this if it involves me," I answered.

Zoe said nothing in response, but the same thesis revealed itself again and shimmied out toward me. I reached up and grabbed it.

"Thanks."

"I don't know if it applies to your situation, but…well, good luck, I suppose. Not the most accessible thing I've written."

"It looks dense."

"It is." Zoe slid into the space beside me, looking down at the spiral-bound thesis. "Not my best work, but it might help you understand what's going on with you in the coming weeks."

"Pardon?"

"Fight or flight responses," Zoe said. "In short, when you have high-level power, your body intuitively understands that you have access to those tools. For example, given the chance, my instinct wants to use my power to solve every problem I run into, but if I don't hold back, then I'll blow apart a city block."

"Got it," I answered. It was close to the truth.

"It's more extreme than that, but that's the gist of it. Though I don't know if it'll apply, considering your base-level power is innocuous and passive."

"You don't know?" I asked.

"Emma doesn't either. Can't memorize everything you read."

I nodded along, even though I managed it most of the time.

"Fine. The rest of us can't memorize everything we read, Toby." Zoe took the thesis from my hands, actually grabbing it with hers, and placed it on one of the few open spots on her desk. Several toys skittered out of the way. "Unfortunately, Emma and I also can't look up information regarding your power unless we want to set off alarm bells."

"And yet you brought me here," I said.

"A girl's gotta know," Zoe shrugged. Did she know how annoyed Emma had been about it? I at least had to assume they knew more about the safety of this stunt than I did.

"Well, now you do," I said.

"Now I do," she affirmed. "Do you remember anything about our conversation thus far?" Zoe brushed away some more of the fidget toys and sat on the desk. A pen and stack of paper that hadn't been there when I'd walked in set to notation. The front page was already half full.

"Have you said anything since the elevator ride?"

Zoe's eyes widened for a flash, but she hid it well. Then she rolled her eyes once she realized I'd caught that. "That's...curious. I couldn't tell at all."

"Couldn't tell?"

"I'm literally in your head, and I didn't know when you stopped time and—and I was talking to another version of you. You're the same. To a degree. Or at least it's an excellent simulacrum."

"I've heard about clones," I pointed out. I was still looking over the bookshelf.

"Clone's heads aren't quite empty, but might as well be. If I look at a clone, the thoughts are there, but nobody's home." Zoe hummed to herself, and the pen stopped writing for a moment. "I couldn't tell at all."

"Weird," I said.

"And you don't remember any of it?" she asked again.

"No."

"This is why I wanted to do this and why it was worth the shit I'm going to get from Emma." The chair on the far side of Zoe's desk pulled itself out. "Take a seat."

I shot one last glance at the hidden books on the bottom shelf before heading over to the chair. Zoe scoffed but didn't comment on me finding them. At least she was trying to keep the conversation even.

For the most part.

"Did you talk to Emma?" Zoe asked once I'd sat down.

"Yes. Found her in her office."

"Which floor were we on?"

"Between seventh and eighth."

"That's 60 feet, give or take," Zoe said, mostly to herself. One toy, a white cube covered in switches, jumped into the air and clicked around for a moment.

Both of the girls were restless. They just fidgeted in different ways.

"Is 60 feet what you expected?"

"No. Emma's power has a longer range. My running theory was that it would match her numbers, but that's not the case."

"So, I need to stay about sixty feet away from her?" I asked. Zoe didn't need to read my mind to catch the obvious disappointment in my voice.

"For now," Zoe said.

Shit. I wanted to follow up on that kiss and—

Zoe cocked her head.

I nodded. "Sixty feet. Got it."

"Good." Zoe didn't lean down, but her desk drawer opened, and a small plastic case hopped up out and onto the desk. The drawer closed itself. "I get it, though. You just found out you're soulmates, and Emma's great. You'll have all the time in the world after we finish."

"Till death do us part?" I suggested.

"Well, either death or we need to ship you off somewhere to avoid triggering your power again. How do you feel about the Southern Hemisphere?"

My stomach dropped.

"Hey, fifty years ago, they would have just killed you." Zoe paused for a little too long. "I'm not condoning that, but it puts a trip to New Zealand under witness protection in context." Zoe's computer sparked to life despite her sitting several feet away. "Either way. All starts with a blood test. That's all we need." I could hear the tone shift in her voice at the end.

"All we need?" I asked.

"Well, there are a couple hundred hours of secret testing between us and freedom, but I was trying to make it sound easy," Zoe said. The plastic case she'd pulled from the desk opened, and a needle popped out. "Okay. Sleeve up."

I complied, but it involved taking off my sweater.

"Arm out," Zoe said. Before I was even in position, an alcohol wipe was cleaning off the needle's target. "We can keep talking. My power will take care of this. I've done it a thousand times."

The needle struck. I hissed.

"Pansy," Zoe scoffed.

"Little hard?" I suggested.

Zoe considered the dent she'd made in my arm as blood flowed. The needle pulled back, resting on my skin instead of pressing into it.

"What are we testing for?" I asked.

"Blood."

"Hilarious."

"Thanks, I'm here most days." Zoe's power flicked the needle. Maybe I had slow blood. "I'm running a simple categorization test first. Should give us some information."

"Are those accurate?" I'd read otherwise.

"Best thing we've got," she said, which didn't answer the question. "It's not perfect, but it's also not the only test I'm running. I'll need some extra blood. Especially because I'll need to use my field test kit."

"Why?"

"Records," Zoe answered. The syringe was almost full. Another pulled itself from the kit. They swapped places, but Zoe was much more gentle this time. "But the field test isn't perfect, so I'll be running them twice."

"Okay, and what does category testing even do for us?" I asked. I'd been in the unrecognized category for my entire life. That was what being an Omega rarity got you.

"There are several categories that we mark as uncategorized, but we know what they are." Zoe took the first syringe she'd filled and replaced the cap before putting it back in the case. "If you fall under some of those, we're in trouble."

"Trouble?"

"If someone falls under one of those categories, they are put under supervision and restriction right away," Zoe explained. "For example, once it was clear how strong I was, they put me in special schools. Paired me up with Emma. Stuff like that."

"Okay."

"In theory, it'd be easy to do that to you because we'd just need to isolate you from Emma, but—"

"—But people can trigger their powers without their soulmate around once they've been exposed," I said, so she didn't have to.

"Nice. Someone paid attention in class."

"Movies," I admitted.

"Fair," Zoe finished the second syringe, and another replaced it. How much blood was she taking? "But yeah, the emotional charge thing puts us in a bind. It's pretty hard to prove that you'd never use your power when: one, you don't know how to control it, and two, separating someone from their soulmate for long periods of time leaves them emotionally charged."

"Awesome."

"Not really," she said. "There is a reason people like that girl outside protest the DPR. Things can get pretty... intense, Toby."

I took a deep breath at that. She was already talking about separating us, and though Zoe was avoiding saying it now, she'd implied killing me earlier.

"You don't get executed for no reason," she cut in. "We do everything in our power to ensure that you have as free a life as possible. I mean, hell, look at me."

"You seem fine."

"Depends who you ask," Zoe said. I didn't prod further into that. "Just one more syringe, and we should be good for everything I need to run."

"Okay," I said. There was quiet in the office for a moment, and it felt like wasted time, so I spoke up. "What's the worst-case scenario?"

"Worst-case?" Zoe asked. Several toys on the desk danced.

"Yes."

"Not pretty," Zoe sighed. "The absolute worst-case is that you're a horseman. That your power leaves some residue on time and erodes it. Crazy stuff like that."

"Horseman?"

"Industry term for a potential world-ender," she explained. "The last two were in Europe, but the definition's gotten more strict over the years. Hell, I would have been one back in the day."

"Does Europe have a thing for world-ending or—" I cut myself off as Zoe frowned.

"Funny as that is," she lied, "that's the worst-case, and we're all doing our best to prove that it isn't what's going on."

"And if it is?"

"Well..."

Zoe looked away. She didn't want to talk about this.

"You're right. I don't," she answered my thoughts.

"Tell me anyway."

"Fine," Zoe sighed. "If it's the case, and you can't stop using your power because of the emotionally charged state..."—a deep breath—"Look, I said it back at DiRezzo's, and I probably shouldn't have. I'll give you a head start."

I swallowed spit. I understood where that ended.

"Yeah. We should hope for the best, but—" Zoe got up off the desk and fumbled around in one drawer. I'd gotten so used to the office self-animating that it was almost weird to see her actively hunt. "Here."

Zoe threw a pocket knife that flicked open. It held in place way too close to my face for comfort.

"Fucking hell."

"I always had it," she said. "Take it."

"A knife?"

"Something to defend yourself with if I end up chasing you," she said, smiling until she read my expression. "Okay, I get it. Not really funny, but keep it. Never know when you might need it."

"For you?"

"Not everyone's as nice as me, Toby."

9

Toby - Ticking Away I

The rules were pretty simple: don't do anything crazy and follow instructions when I got a text from Zoe or Emma. Until then, it was back to living life quietly for a few days—or at least as long as it took Zoe to run the tests. In her words, they took a while.

I'd also confirmed that Zoe'd taken care of my job by getting me let go. I wasn't surprised, per se, but if there weren't much more pressing matters, I would have been pissed. I at least had to assume she had a plan unless she was planning for Emma to pay the bills for the rest of my life.

At least the firing made sense if there was an investigation into my powers. You couldn't have a world-ender selling insurance. That was insider trading.

That said, going from salesman to trophy husband, I'd heard of worse trajectories.

They'd told me to act normal, so I was meeting Todd at a cocktail bar to say goodbye to the old job. At least, I was supposed to be. At the moment, I was outside on the phone with my mother, who'd called as soon as I'd texted her about it.

"Yeah, Mom, I'm fine," I said for the seventh time in this conversation.

"Are you sure, honey?" she said over the phone. There was clinking on her end. A spoon on ceramic. Knowing Mom, it was tea. "I thought you liked your job," she continued.

"I was good at it," I corrected.

"You sound sad," she said. The stirring stopped. "Are you sad?"

"No."

"Don't lie to me."

"I'm not lying. I'd know if I was lying. I have—"

"And I have a mother's intuition."

"Mom. I'm fine."

"Then you're keeping something from me," she said. I closed my eyes for a bit longer than a standard blink. The cocktail bar door opened as a woman left.

"No."

"How's everything with you and Dad?"

"Florida's nice."

"How's the tea?"

"It's coffee for your father."

"Coffee?"

"Decaf," she said. "What are you hiding?"

"Nothing."

"Is it a girl?"

"No." That was a harder lie. Before, I'd only been omitting.

"Oh my god, it is." She put one hand over the phone like it'd keep me from hearing her. "Robert, Toby found a girl!"

I might have had my powers, but she was a mother. Evenly matched. "Mom."

My dad said something in the background, and my cellphone garbled it enough that even I couldn't make it out.

"Your father's asking if she's cute."

I'd caught enough to understand that wasn't how he'd worded it. "I don't wanna get into it yet," I said as an excuse. "It's early. Don't break out the champagne." I almost winced at the latter part. That was what we should have been doing.

"Well, it's okay, even if she isn't. A nice girl is a nice girl." A brief pause. "No sudden spikes in power?"

"No, Mom." Lucky for me and my battle against a mother's

intuition. That wasn't a lie. My power hadn't spiked. It had transformed.

"Well, don't let that get to you. Your father and I—"

"Hey, Mom," I cut her off before she hiked up the path of one of her usual lectures. "I'm meeting Todd right now for drinks because of the job thing. I don't want to keep him waiting."

"Oh! Say hi to him for me!"

"I will."

"And Toby," she said, "if you're not busy, come visit." I could hear her perking up on the other end of the phone. I hadn't been down south to see them for two years. I'd always used work as the reason, which meant I'd lost my excuse.

"I'll see if I can make it. Love you." I waited for her to hang up. I didn't want that to be a lie, but I had to figure out everything with my power first. I felt like being a world-ender plopped you onto the no-fly list, especially if I was supposed to stay separated from Emma.

Then again, maybe a sunny Florida retirement community was far enough away from Crescent to count. All the ladies there would find me suave when I noticed their hair had gotten whiter.

I shoved my phone into my pocket and heard it click against the handle of Zoe's knife. It was weird and heavy, having something extra in my pockets. I'd gotten used to a routine of phone, wallet, and keys. Everything else usually went into a bag, but I didn't figure I'd have time to unzip if I had to use the knife.

Todd was already at the table with two drinks. The one on my side was a toxic green color I didn't appreciate. He waved, and I slipped between the too-close seating arrangements to make my way over to him.

All the art on the walls had little tags at the bottom, noting how much they were to purchase. There wasn't a single reasonable price in the place.

"There he is!" Todd said once I'd almost sat down. "What took you? Don't say work."

"Mom called. She says hi."

"How's Sharon?"

"Nosy."

"She's a mom, that's her right."

"Yeah." I shrugged. The drink in front of me couldn't have been healthy. "Do I want to know what's in this?"

"You'll know once you taste."

"I'm not sure I want to taste."

"Come on," Todd said, "don't invite me out for drinks, and then turn down the drinks."

I pushed the drink an inch further away from me. "I didn't invite you out. You told me we were coming here."

"You told me you lost your job. Same thing." He reached across and grabbed my cocktail, swapping it with his, sipped but less toxic-looking one. "Sorry about that, by the way."

"It was soul-sucking," I offered.

"Most jobs are, but we need 'em." He took a sip of the drink he'd bought me and winced. He swapped the drinks back. "Does Emma know?"

"No."

"When are you gonna tell her?"

"When we talk," I suggested. The stance was that, officially, I hadn't spoken to her. Depending on how you counted stopped time, I had never spoken to Emma at all.

"You haven't talked to her yet?"

I shook my head.

"Dude, I asked you not to fuck this up for me. Text her right now."

"I'm not texting her right now."

"What are you thinking, the three-day rule thing people say? That stuff's bullshit."

"I'll talk to her soon."

"You might have blown your shot. She's even more out of your league now," Todd said.

"Even more?"

"You lost your job."

"And she was out of my league before?" I asked.

"Have you seen her?"

"Fair." I considered the drink again but didn't take it. The music in the bar changed to something a little easier to speak over.

"I'm not forgetting. Text Emma right now."

"Todd."

"Toby," he mocked.

"I'm not texting her right now. I don't want to start a conversation when I'm about to be drunk," I said. It was a bullshit reason. I just wasn't supposed to text her, but Todd nodded.

Then he looked at the drink. God dammit.

I grabbed the glass and steeled myself. The things I did for love. I took the first sip. It burned, but the color was worse than the taste.

Todd laughed. "I've had that one. Soo and I were here last week. Back in a sec." He stammered it all out in one breath before pushing out from his chair and heading to the washroom.

In retrospect. Telling Todd that I'd gotten fired was 'acting natural,' but there was no way that coming out for drinks was being responsible with everything going on. I'd need to find an excuse to pull the parachute cord early and head home.

I took out my phone and opened my new contact for Emma. Zoe'd given me her number, but we didn't have a message history. After a second, I sighed and turned my phone off to ensure I didn't do anything stupid after an ounce or two of liquid courage.

I recognized a voice. "I'm good, thanks. Don't need the attention tonight."

I turned and saw the girl who'd been canvassing outside of the DPR in the morning. She caught me looking before I thought of avoiding her for secrecy's sake.

"Hi," I said once her eyes widened for a moment. "How'd everything wrap up?"

"It's—um—fine. How was the meeting?"

"Also fine, I guess," I said. Now that I was in the conversation, I might as well be friendly. "What's your name?"

"Pardon?"

"Your name."

"I'd prefer not to."

"Fair," I conceded, especially considering I'd just heard her turn someone away. "I just already gave you mine, but have a nice…" There was a barrier between us, just barely translucent and silver. She must have been on the defensive. "Night," I finished.

"You too."

"Have you texted Emma yet?" Todd wrested my attention back.

"No."

"And you haven't had more either." Todd nodded to the drink. "Toby."

"Todd," I echoed his earlier pattern. "I was just talking to—" I turned, but in the seconds I'd been talking to Todd, the girl had left the bar. No bill, nothing. Just gone. Plus, she'd been sitting alone…

"Who?"

"Yeah," I said, which wasn't a response.

The barrier had been strange. And now this? What was going on? Who was that girl? Crescent was a big city. Running into someone twice in the same day was—I shook my head; coincidences happened. I must have just been on edge from…well, everything else going on.

"How you doing upstairs, buddy?" Todd asked.

I snapped back to him. "Just distracted."

"You?" Todd sat back down. "Okay, you gotta text her."

"Just a second." How many people had been in the bar before? Multiple people had left when she did. What was…

"Toby."

"Just a second, Todd," I repeated. Todd retreated, and I got up from my chair. Five people. Five people had left when Todd had come back. The people behind the bar were talking amongst themselves. No bills. No evidence. Just gone.

Coincidences happened. Was I willing to bet that this was one?

"I need air," I said. Todd almost spoke up, but I was already walking toward the back door. There was a warning on it, letting me know that an alarm would activate if it opened, but I'd seen someone use it out of the corner of my eye when Todd was saying hi.

I pushed out into the cool night air. The door closed behind me a second later. Just me and yellow streetlamps on either side of the alleyway.

Was I going crazy? Zoe'd told me to act normal, to avoid doing anything crazy. This was doing something crazy. This was going to make Todd ask about me at work. This was going to...

To my right, on the side of the alleyway closer to the cocktail bar's normal entrance, a man was staring me down. Shadows were covering his face, but he was watching.

Fuck coincidences.

I started in the other direction, walking quick to avoid drawing too much attention as I pulled my phone out. I checked my shoulder. The man was still there, staring.

I just needed to text Zoe that something was going on and—

My phone was off. Of course. Fuck.

I reached the end of the alleyway and shot another glance back. The man was following now, a deliberate march. That confirmed it. I was 100% being watched. I took a deep breath and went to turn away from the bar.

A translucent barrier. Almost invisible in the night. It probably was to anyone other than me.

"Toby Vander," the canvasser said. There was more confidence in her voice here. "Mind if we have a few words?"

Oh shit. Oh—

"Who the fuck are you?" Todd asked. I turned and saw the girl glare at Todd. Even without super strength, Todd was over six feet tall and built like a truck. She stared him down anyway.

"You're not part of this," she said before turning back to me. I stepped toward her, away from the barrier blocking my path. "Toby. Just a few—"

"The fuck I'm not," Todd said. He loomed over the woman but didn't make a move. Todd wasn't a violent guy, and even beyond that, you couldn't tell much about someone based on size alone.

"Todd, just don't—" The man who'd been walking up the alleyway behind me was close now, and there were three more in my peripheral vision. We were surrounded. Who were these people? What was going on?

"He's right. Don't." The girl took another step toward me.

Todd put a hand on the girl's shoulder. She didn't flinch, but he pulled her attention for a second.

"Run!" I yelled as I dove to the side. The man out in the middle of the street was the smallest. You couldn't tell much based on size, but it was all I had.

Todd didn't run. He wound up.

I'd seen Todd hit someone in the past. They'd flown ten feet. This girl didn't budge.

Todd swore. The girl kept her eyes on me.

I found my footing after the dive and steadied myself on the curb. The man I'd started toward raised an arm, and the ground beneath my feet froze, turning slick and impossible. I ate the dirt. Or at least ice. "Todd! Run. Get Zo—" I managed before the wind got knocked out of me.

"Shit." I heard Todd swear. I went to crawl, but another barrier was in front of my nose.

"God dammit," the girl spat. "Leave the other one. Don't fuck this up more than we already have."

I tried to find my footing, but the ice was still on the ground.

The night was never quite silent in Crescent, but a crashing boom shattered over the entire street. I heard the glass of streetlamps crack.

"Fuck," the girl hissed.

I felt the familiar sizzle of Zoe's power against my skin.

"All right," Zoe called out to the group spread out across the street. "You're all coming with me. Field Suppression Agent Zoe

McCourtney. I would suggest you comply."

I felt her power wrap around my chest, almost like a hand. It pulled me to my feet and held me steady on the ice. I saw Todd raise his hands behind the girl.

The canvasser was staring daggers at Zoe. "We just need to talk to him."

"Looks like duress to me," Zoe said. She'd know. "Toby. How'd you get into trouble so quick?"

"I must have a knack for it," I said. Todd's eyes jumped between us. We were being a little too familiar.

Zoe dropped from the sky, landing in the middle of the street, surrounded like I was. "You okay?" she asked.

"Think so," I said.

Zoe nodded, then took two steps toward the girl, cracking her neck to either side as she did. "All right. Let's make this easy an—"

The canvasser cut her off, throwing her hands forward and raising a metallic wall that threw itself toward Zoe. Zoe shifted to the side, dragged by her power instead of walking or running. She was hovering several inches above the concrete now.

"See," Zoe brushed herself off to emphasize that she hadn't gotten hit. "That's resisting arrest." I could feel the air pressure rise as Zoe glared at the woman. "Now I don't need to play nice."

I heard the crackle behind me, and a bolt of pure ice streaked toward Zoe's head. Before I could shout, the ice smashed itself into powder, scattering around Zoe in a harmless flurry. The telepath took a deep breath.

"If you wanna dance, we can dance." Zoe raised a hand, and I heard a yelp. I turned and saw the man who'd been shooting ice rise into the air. "Just a fair warning. I prefer to lead."

Zoe turned her attention back to the barrier girl, and there was a sickening snap as the man's arm shattered above me.

10

Zoe - Ticking Away II

I let go, and the man dropped, screaming. I still couldn't hear the thoughts of the girl in front of me, but the others backed away. That was how it usually went. You just needed to show people how uneven the fight would be, and they'd back off.

The girl's eyes narrowed. At least one of them had a spine. Either that or a lack of common sense.

I bounced back and forth on my feet for a second before my power caught me, picking me up off the ground and holding me in the air. Flying wasn't the easiest thing, considering I was more holding myself in freefall than flying, but nothing beat being able to move in three dimensions.

The girl shot another glance at Toby. I matched it.

"You get out of here," I said to him. For a half-second, Toby hesitated. Todd didn't. "Now."

Todd grabbed Toby. He'd seen what I could do. From Toby's perspective, they had me surrounded and outnumbered. He'd been trying to think of a way to help, but I didn't need it.

Surrounded? Sure. Outnumbered? Certainly. Outgunned? Hell no.

The girl turned her attention to Toby again, so I waved a hand at her. A shockwave of mental force cascaded down the street before crashing into her chest. I felt my power dissipate against her, but there was still enough force to throw her several feet off the ground and a dozen back. She crashed down onto the pavement, and I heard the metallic scraping of metal instead of skin.

"A shield?" I asked. "Is that why you're so cocky?"

"Fuck you," the girl spat as she got back to her feet. The man with the broken arm was still writhing on the ground.

"This is your last chance to come quietly," I said. I felt my power hiss at my fingertips as I made the offer. I could hear the thoughts of the others. They were close to giving in, but there was a part of me that wanted to let loose. Part of me that wanted them to take a swing so I could drop the hammer on them. It had been so long since I'd taken the leash off.

The four that weren't screaming about their arm closed in.

"No takers. Really?" I asked as I closed my eyes. I could feel them approaching. Feel each step and breath they took as they psyched themselves up for a fight. I could hear their surface thoughts, wondering what I could do to them and how fast they needed to be. "Nobody?" I asked one last time. "What are you all so afraid of?"

No takers. Their thoughts gave that much away.

"And why isn't it me?"

They'd had plans, but I was faster. My power coiled around a leg and lashed out at the kneecap. Before the man had time to feel the pain, I pulled him by the same leg, whipping him across the street and into the window of a nearby cocktail bar.

People had been gawking. Now they were screaming.

The group surrounding me's heads snapped to follow their friend, and I shot up into the air. The girl was probably the only one here who could take a hit and—

I slammed into something in the air, cracking my back against it and losing my hold on myself. I fell to the concrete, only stopping an inch above the ground as my power intervened. What the hell was that?

There wasn't time.

One of the women, a blonde, yelled and slammed her hands into the ground. I felt static singe my skin, and I dragged myself to the side. I was barely several feet away when a flash of lightning seared my eyes, crashing down where I'd been.

I tried to blink away the blindness as my power righted me in the air, stabilizing my stance. It didn't matter how much I shook my head. My eyes were stuck in searing white.

Unfortunately for them, I'd never needed my eyes.

The blonde woman went to slam her hands into the ground again, but I felt her first and grabbed her wrists. She screamed as I sent her flying toward the shield girl. The blonde cracked against her, but she didn't move.

I felt the man with the broken arm getting up off the ground, and I wrapped my thoughts around him again. Pulling him back to the middle of the street. I tied my power around his leg and—

Searing heat behind me.

I dropped to the ground and barely dodged as fire roared above me, crackling through the air and crashing down the street.

"Ain't this a mess?" a man asked.

I knew that voice. It took a moment, but I blinked away the blindness and focused in on the source.

"Kris," I spat. "It's been a while."

"McCourtney," the man said while offering a curt nod. Kris Allens. Pyroportation. Omega Psi. Went to the same class as me in our little locked away school, but more than any of that in the past two years, the leader of The Red. The anti-regulation terrorist group.

But if all the people here were part of the Red, then what the hell did they want with Toby? "Didn't think I was catching a big fish tonight."

Kris smirked, and the ever-burning embers in his eyes flashed bright for a moment. Fire danced up and down his arms, a harsh contrast against his dark skin. "And I didn't think I'd have this much trouble trying to talk to someone. World's full of disappointments."

My hand was almost vibrating with anticipation. My power knew what this meant. It meant a proper fight. A proper test. Life. Death. "Why would you want to talk to that guy?" I nodded back in the direction Toby'd run. I wanted to fight. I wanted to swing now, but the longer I took, the more time Toby had to get away and the more people could run screaming out of the cocktail bar.

Kris cocked his head at my question. "You don't know?"

I shrugged, easier to lie with body language.

"This really is unfortunate then," Kris said.

"Life's unfortunate. We deal with it."

"Can we get back to what matters here?" the shielded girl asked. I half-raised a hand, but Kris matched me on the draw. We both held fire.

"Who's the bucket of sunshine?"

"Lexi," the girl hissed. She wasn't that much younger than Kris, but her willingness to give a name told me she was new to this.

"Well, Lexi," I said, "you've been a pain in my ass. So let's get back to what matters."

"A pain in the ass?" Kris asked. "You have no idea." He took a step forward, and the same shimmering shield that was wrapped around Lexi crawled across his skin. His thoughts vanished from my head.

Oh shit.

I threw my hands forward, and a shockwave crashed down the street again, throwing cars and bending streetlamps. Kris shot fire into the air and then vanished into a shower of sparks. Lexi raised her arms and a silvery wall formed in front of her. A sedan smashed into it, metal shattering against the barrier.

Kris reformed above me, sparks scattering out of the fire and coalescing into a man. I wrapped my power around the sedan I'd just crashed against Lexi's shield and threw it up toward him. He disappeared into another shower of sparks as flames engulfed the car. I dove to the side as it came crashing back down to earth, but ended up slamming into another barrier. In the second I lashed out with my power instead, sending the falling car careening into the signage of the cocktail bar. Neon light and sparks poured out into the street.

Kris reformed in the building fire I'd just started.

Where were the other people that'd been with them? Two were running the wrong way, but—

Toby.

I shot off to chase after the man running in that direction, but a barrier popped up in front of me again. I called my power from further down the street, building a tsunami of force from a block away, pulling cars from their parking spots, and bending street signs. As it got closer, several sedans went flying. One of them landed on one of Lexi's allies that'd been trying to scurry away.

I grabbed the wave of thought just before it reached me and focused it into a shot, cracking it toward Lexi's chest. The power slammed into her and—

Broke against her, scarring the street on either side of her but leaving her unharmed.

What the hell? It'd just worked a minute ago. I'd knocked her back even though—

A torrent of fire poured toward me and I threw myself to the ground, smashing into the asphalt to avoid the flames. I heard the telltale sound of Kris popping into existence above me.

My power wrapped around a streetlamp and tore it from the sidewalk, throwing concrete and stone into the air as I swung it like a bat, cracking against Kris's spine. The streetlamp broke instead of him, but the force still sent him flying.

I swore. The fire was spreading. Kris was gaining avenues of attack and I didn't know how to make progress here.

My power grabbed me before I could climb back to my feet, literally picking me up and righting me. Pain shot across my chest. I'd cracked a rib before. I knew what it felt like.

Kris flashed back into existence on top of the car I'd embedded in a wall. Lexi walked up in the middle of the street. The broken-armed man that'd chased after Todd and Toby was well out of range. Shit.

Behind me, I felt the blonde woman trying to slam her hands into the ground again. Just when she was about to touch the earth I grabbed her wrists again, this time I pulled hard. Too hard. She screamed. That was fine. This wasn't about her.

"Neat trick, Kris," I said as the man dusted himself off on top of the broken car.

"Had to even the playing field somehow."

"You're going down, bitch," Lexi hissed. She looked disheveled. Off balance. Her breath was haggard. If nothing else, I was making her work for it.

"Where've you been hiding?" I asked. I was panting the same way she was, but that was probably just the rib. "Thought I'd know about someone like you."

"Ain't soulmates a bitch?" she asked.

Kris's eyes went wide.

"Oh, you *are* new," I snapped as I charged forward through the air. The girl raised her hands to throw up a barrier, but I was already prepared, banking to the right around the shimmering shield. She tried to pivot as I ended up beside her, but it was too late.

I couldn't hit her, but she had to stand on something.

My power ran through the cracks in the street and found purchase, tearing at the earth and shattering the asphalt under her. Water rushed as pipes burst. The sidewalk caved as I pulled away at it.

Lexi went flying as I slammed her and the ground she'd been standing on into an empty office building, caving in the third floor and—

Fire flashed next to me and I slipped out of the way just as it shattered into sparks and reformed into Kris's deadly glare. He held up a palm. I pulled on the sedan in the wall.

The flames were faster but got cut off by steel. Kris slammed into the ground, imprinting on the street, and I smelled my hair burning.

Too close for comfort, but that was it. I'd come back and clean this up in a minute. Right now, Toby needed my help.

I also needed a doctor, but there was an order of operations to follow.

A piece of the broken sign fell off the building, crashing into the ground just short of the hole I'd left in the street and sidewalk. Dammit. I'd really made a mess this time.

I took two steps as a running start for takeoff. My power grabbed me to take off like a shot and—

I cracked against a barrier that erupted from the ground in front of me. My arm crumpled in on itself and I screamed as it caved in. Blood shot out from my fingertips and I felt heat beside me.

They were alive. I was just so used to hearing the thoughts of people I was fighting that—

Oh God. Emma.

Kris flashed into existence from sparks beside me and held out a hand as I dropped to my knees.

"Sorry, always wished I'd been able to convince you."

Emma.

"Goodbye, Zoe."

11
Toby - Ticking Away III

My feet were moving faster than I thought they could carry me as Todd dragged me along the busy street. His powers might not have made him a speeder, but my weight on his arm was nothing to him, and each of his strides was powerful enough to send us flying several feet. Zoe'd told him to get us away, and he was succeeding.

"Todd." I shoved against him as he dragged me. I tried to wiggle, and he slowed.

"Fucking what?" he snapped. It echoed off the buildings of the dark street, coming back at us like a physical force.

"We have to go back and—"

"Are you kidding me?" he asked.

Fire shot into the sky back where we'd come from, illuminating that end of the street in a hellish glow. Zoe was in over her head. I went to take a step backward. Todd stopped me halfway through it.

"Zoe doesn't need *your* help, Toby."

"I can help."

"How? Watching it really well?" Todd asked. "Dude. You don't spend time around this. I work with Zoe. I've seen her numbers. The last thing she needs is you and me—" Todd lost his breath and doubled over. "Fuck," he coughed, "I'm out of shape."

"There were five of them," I said.

"I only saw four," Todd answered, "but I'll take your number." He took a moment to rally himself. There were sirens in the distance, just starting to overpower the cities' natural cacophony. Todd continued, "Four is child's play for Zoe. She's fine."

"Yeah." I stared back at the scene we'd left. This was my fault. This was all my fault. If she got hurt... she was just trying to help me.

Why had those people been trying to pull me like that?

"We should get moving." Todd coughed one more time. "God, I need to get back to the gym."

"You have a treadmill at home, don't you?"

"That's Soo's."

I pulled my arm away from Todd and paced for a moment, my shoes scraping against the cracked sidewalk. "I just think we s—" I was cut off as an earth-shattering sound wave crashed down the street, shattering windows and setting off car alarms before it kicked me in the chest. It wasn't enough to wind me, but it stung. "What was that?"

"See, that's Zoe for you. She's fine." Todd sounded confident, but I didn't know if he was right. That couldn't have been her holding back, and based on what she'd told me, she wouldn't let loose unless something was seriously wrong.

Zoe's power echoed down the street again. I stared. "What if something happens?"

"Toby,"—Todd grabbed my shoulders—"you saw those people. You've seen Zoe. What are *we* going to do there?"

"I'm calling Emma."

"You're calling her for the first time now?" Todd snapped.

"Just—" I held up a hand to shut him up. I didn't want to explain everything to Todd. The phone was ringing, but she wasn't answering.

Todd was right. I couldn't help. Not like this. But if I had Emma? If I could stop time?

An explosion rumbled down the street, and I watched dust fly up from the buildings. There wasn't a person inside the smoke, so at least I knew Zoe hadn't gotten thrown around. Todd had gotten distracted. If I ran now—

"Toby, what the hell?!" Todd yelled as I took off the street toward Zoe. I couldn't let someone I barely knew fight for me, especially when I didn't know what she was going against. It didn't matter that it was her job. It didn't matter that she was stronger than me. What mattered was that she was my soulmate's best friend and one of the two people on my side in this world.

Emma's answering machine picked up. Shit.

A shadow came into the street, silhouetted against the red glow of the building fire back where we'd started. The sidewalk turned slick, and my steps turned into a slide again. After careening for several feet, I ended up on my ass, smashing my tailbone on the concrete. Ice and snow ate my palms as I slid to a stop.

A wincing, hooded, dark-haired man was in the street, one arm hanging limp at his side.

I tried to jump to my feet, but ice climbed up my leg and affixed me to the ground. The man pulled down his hood, and his thick-rimmed glasses flashed in the streetlight. He approached. "We did just want to talk, Toby." His words were haggard and stilted. Broken arm.

"Who are you even?"

"Can't talk here," he managed. He kept his gaze on me as he spoke. "We don't want to hurt you." He was being honest.

But I could fill in the second part myself: 'but we will if we have to.'

The man offered his unbroken hand, and I felt the ice on my ankle retreat. "Come on," he said.

"I—" Emma and Zoe'd said I'd be in danger because of my power, but I hadn't considered this. I didn't understand how they knew, what they knew, or who they were. Either way, I didn't reach out to take his hand.

The man scoffed.

Todd's dark fist slammed into the man's cheek. There was a half-second when everything almost happened in slow motion. Blue ice formed on the man's face as Todd cracked through it. The man took off like a shot, snapping to the side and flying across the street into the door of a red sedan.

"The fuck are you doing, Toby?" Todd asked.

"You again? Christ," the man said as he staggered off the ground. Ice formed around the man's feet, and the dented car rose off the street.

Todd reached down and broke the last of the ice wrapped around my ankle.

I yanked Todd to the pavement by his collar.

The sedan flew over us, smashing into the brickwork behind. Dust sprayed into the street, and I rolled to the side before finding my feet again. It took Todd several more seconds.

We had to get out of here.

I had to help Zoe.

I needed more time.

I—

I held out a hand and tried to focus. The man dusted off his jacket and swore to himself. I felt Todd grab my shoulder.

Nothing. I couldn't do it.

"Last chance to come quietly," the man said. His eyes were ice blue but still burning into me.

Todd let go of my shoulder, and I stayed squared up to the man. Todd had the right idea. He should run. This didn't involve him.

The man was panting. Each breath crystallized ice in the air. I couldn't imagine getting thrown into a car when you'd already broken an arm felt good.

I kept staring him down.

"Fine," he finally spat. The man raised a hand.

I jumped to keep myself from getting caught in the ice forming on the ground. Just as I was about to come crashing down onto it, it disappeared. There was a flash of red to my right as the poor sedan flew across the street, crashing into the man's legs as he tried to jump to the side.

I ran at him. It was the only thing I could do.

The ice man flailed as I ended up on top of him. He was already bleeding from a cut on his forehead, looking dizzy or worse. I pushed away his one good arm, shoving it down into the sidewalk. He'd use his power if he could focus again, and then we were back in trouble.

I used my free hand to grab Zoe's knife from my pocket. I struggled to get it open before pressing it against his chest. "Don't move," I choked out.

He didn't respond.

My hands were shaking, and I tried to keep the knife steady. I just needed to keep him down. I didn't have to do anything drastic. I could hold him here, and someone would come. After all, he'd been trying to kill us. This was all self-defense and—

The man's pale blue eyes shifted back to the cold of ice as they refocused. A freezing chill over my skin. I moved the knife up to his neck. I could feel his pulse. I could—

His arm shot up.

I pressed down.

I was faster.

Blood welled over the knife as I broke skin, and the cold dropped away as I held the steel in his throat. He was choking. The red poured over my hands. Oh God. I—I dropped the knife. There were bubbles of air coming out of the gash in his throat.

I scrambled backward off him. I was covered in blood. There was so much. It was everywhere. He wasn't dead, he was just dying and—

I needed to get away. I needed this to be over. I needed this to stop. I needed—

"JUST STOP!"

The fucking world listened.

I staggered to my feet, the oncoming police lights locked in place, bathing half the street in distant red and half in faded blue. There was a body on the ground in front of me. Blood pooled around them, smooth and rippleless. Todd was behind me, reaching out, trying to grab the space where I'd just been standing.

Down the street, back where Zoe had been, the firelight bled into the mixed colors of the police beacons, overpowering it as the street turned into a climbing inferno.

I took another look back at Todd, his face screwed in panic, the blood staining his chest. When had he gotten hurt? Was he going to be okay?

My hands were shaking again.

I took another deep breath and headed down the street toward Zoe. I walked slowly between the plumes of smoke and over the shattered glass. I had all the time in the world, after all.

There was an impossible quiet on the street. The world around me was a tableau of chaos, but I could hear my footsteps, my breathing, and my racing heart. Halfway there, I realized I had Zoe's knife in my hand, locked in a white-knuckle grip. I shoved it into my pocket without wiping it off. I felt the blood seep into the fabric.

Along the street, cars were thrown about and overturned, blocking my vision of what was going on further down. The first thing I saw when I passed the last blue truck was a body.

One of the men who had surrounded me in the alleyway was splattered in front of me, crushed under a twisted sedan. His blood reflected what should have been shimmering firelight.

Nothing shimmered here. The light was flat and lifeless.

What was here? Blood. Rubble. Broken cars.

Zoe.

Zoe was in the middle of the street, on her hands and knees. Her clothes were torn and burned. Her face was covered in a mix of drying and pouring blood. Her fire-red hair was matted and twisted.

A man was looming over her, holding his hand out. I could see the embers flickering at his fingers.

Zoe was going to die.

She was—

No. She wouldn't. I could do something about this. I could finally do something about this.

I ran over to Zoe even though part of me understood that time

didn't matter. I grabbed her arm, and just when I was about to pull...
I froze.

What was this going to do?

How would this work?

What was—

Did it matter?

I grabbed Zoe, heaving her onto my weakened shoulders. She was lighter than I expected, but still dead weight in this timeless place. Zoe slumped against me, and it took a second to find my footing, but I did.

One last look at the man who'd been about to kill her. His placid face. His dark skin.

I stole Zoe away from her fate. I didn't know what would get rewritten, but it would be worth it.

12

Toby - Broken Clocks

I laid Zoe's unblinking form on the ground, giving myself a break now that we were several blocks away from the carnage. We were safe. Or at least safer. I didn't know what was happening on the other side of all this. There was another version of me out there. Was there another version of her?

It was strange, being on a soundless waterfront. I'd been on the docks in the crowdless late night before, but never without the ever-present sound of waves. At the moment, the only thing I heard was my breath and my heartbeat. Maybe those were the only things I'd ever hear again.

I'd managed to drag Zoe to a quiet part of the pier. The evening crowds had either scattered from the chaos back in the city or headed somewhere with better nightlife. Now, I just needed to figure out how to un-stop this. There wasn't an Emma to separate from. I was stuck here.

The solution that made the most sense was that I had to avoid being 'emotionally charged.' My powers were a clenched fist, and I just needed to relax, to let go. But how was I supposed to do that while looking at Zoe's panicked eyes... At the wide, frozen fear locked on her face. At the bloody hair matted to her cheek. She'd been about to die.

What about the blood on my hands? I...I'd killed someone.

I pulled Zoe's knife out of my pocket. It was still damp.

Fuck.

I threw the knife to the Pacific, but the air caught it first, stopping it in time several inches from my fingers. It lingered halfway through the throw, glistening in a time-locked beam of moonlight. A sliver of silver light shone through the bloodstains on the handle. "Ah fuck off," I sighed.

I grabbed the knife from the air. Everything was still here. Peaceful. I could see each facet of moon and city lights on the water caught in the middle of its dance on the waves. I knew it was impossible for light to work like that. Almost like I was standing in a picture instead of reality.

Zoe screamed.

I snapped around as lights flashed across the pier, time catching up in a single breath before I was staring at the telepath on the ground. She was screaming her lungs raw and digging her nails into her cheek.

Shooting pain cascaded up my arm, and I felt it displace, my shoulder cracking in directions it shouldn't. I went to scream, but a hand of force wrapped around my throat. My legs gave out, but I stayed floating in the air, supported by the neck alone.

I couldn't breathe. I tried to use my good arm to claw at my throat, but I hit skin before anything that could have been grabbing me. "Zoe," I squeaked.

My heartbeat rang in my ears. Darkness crept in on the edge of my vision. Zoe's screams sounded distant.

"Zoe, please."

I felt my grip slack, and I dropped the knife. Metal clattered on the pier.

I followed, my knees cracking against the wood. I tried to take in air faster, too fast, and just ended up coughing on my hands and knees.

"I'm..." Zoe sat up, her face still cut and her hair matted to her face. "I'm alive?"

I tried to respond, but my breaths were too staggered and shaking.

"Toby." Zoe went to crawl over to me but put weight on a shattered arm; she tumbled to the pier. For a second, before the pain caught up with her, she seemed almost shocked that she'd been able to fall.

"Zoe," I coughed. I reached out but didn't quite have the strength to get over to her yet.

The girl spent a moment on the ground before using her good arm to push herself off the floor. Her eyes widened as she looked around the pier. Sweat started dripping into the blood on her forehead. "No, no, no, no, no," she stammered, "this is wrong. This is wrong."

"Zoe." I found the wherewithal to get over to her and at least get a hand on her shoulder. "It's okay. You're—"

"Toby. I died. I'm—This is wrong. I died."

"Zoe, you're not."

"I died," she repeated, her voice cracked, and two of the nearby boards on the pier joined it, splintering from a random lash of her power. "I remember. I..." Zoe's hand drifted back to her right cheek, her nails digging into the skin and leaving red angry lines "The fire. I was on—"

"Zoe." I grabbed her hand and pulled it from her face. She turned and stared at me for a moment, her blue eyes empty and glassy. She blinked once.

Twice.

Zoe's eyes focused on mine.

"What did you do?" she asked.

"I—" That was a good question. "I don't know. It looked like you were in danger, so I pulled you away and brought you here while—"

"Toby, I died." She grabbed my shoulder with her one working hand. I hissed at it and pulled away. I didn't know when it'd gotten hurt, but it felt like it was on fire. Zoe's hand stayed in the air for a moment after letting go, then she let it drift back down. "I remember."

"What?"

"I remember it," she repeated. "Everything that happened. My arm. The fire. Kris. Then…" she looked down at the pier, then at her bloody, mangled hand. "Nothing," she whispered, "then nothing."

I felt like a broken record, so I grabbed Zoe's good hand with mine before speaking. "What?"

"Toby, I was dead. I shouldn't be here. I shouldn't…" she trailed off.

"But you are. You're okay. We'll get to a hospital and we'll get fixed up and—" I looked past Zoe for a moment, out toward the city we'd left behind. The flames had died down, but I could see the police lights dancing across most of the core. "I'm glad you're okay. Okay?"

Zoe hesitated long enough that I knew she wasn't being honest. "Okay."

"How's the arm?" I asked. There were…implications to everything she'd been saying, but for the time being, we could focus on the physical.

"Fine," she lied.

"Move it?"

"No." Zoe tried to stand up, but couldn't find the strength in her legs. She closed her eyes for a second and then said, "I can't feel it."

"What?"

"My power, my mind," she explained. "I can't feel it right now. I would normally pick myself off the ground here, but…" She closed her eyes again and took a deep, shaking breath. "Nothing."

"It's there," I said. "You broke part of the pier, and you had me pretty good there."

"Sorry."

"You're a scary woman, Zoe." I took a second to steel myself. My shoulder was screaming, my lungs were burning, and despite it, I needed to be the strong one. I let go of Zoe and pushed myself off the ground, standing up on the pier. "Do you think you're okay to walk?" I asked.

"I don't know what…how," she said. She'd checked into the

conversation for a moment, but her voice was distant again, almost like she was only half here.

"All right, come on." I bent over and grabbed her by the good elbow, helping her stagger absently to her feet. As I did, Zoe put her hand into her pocket. I heard something click in there. Zoe stopped putting effort into standing up, and exhausted as I was, I dropped to the boardwalk with her. My knees smashed against the wood for the second time this evening.

Fuck. Everything hurt so much.

"Zoe, we need to get to—" As I spoke, the air to our right, toward the city, split open, shining brilliant vermillion for a moment before—

"On the ground! Now. Back away!" The voice came before the form, a shadow coming out of the flashing light, then a woman holding out her hand toward me.

I wasn't fast, but I separated myself from Zoe.

A second flash appeared in the air, and a man joined the woman. I recognized the uniform from Zoe. The Department of Power Control.

The woman, a deadly-looking brunette, kept her hand leveled at me while the man, a bulky bearded officer, scanned the surroundings.

I put my good hand up.

Zoe stared at the floor.

"Clear," the man said as he tapped his ear.

There was a third vermillion flash in the air. This time I recognized the man coming through it despite the lack of a uniform, a man with sharp cheeks and glowing eyes that matched the portals that'd just appeared in the air.

Callum Rehsman.

It almost seemed like the waves died as he arrived, leaving his footsteps as the only sound as he approached us on the ground. He barely glanced my way, but I still caught the look. "McCourtney," he said after a moment. "I thought I was coming here to pick up a corpse." Rehsman's hands were still deep in his pockets as he looked down at the crumpled telepath.

Zoe didn't respond.

"And who might you be?" Rehsman asked without as much as glancing my way.

"Toby," I said after a little too long.

"Do you know who this is?" he asked.

I nodded.

"And who we are?"

I nodded again, softer this time.

"And what do you have to do with this?" he asked. "You haven't run upon seeing us, and you certainly aren't the one who hurt McCourtney here. I'd know about you if you were capable of that."

Part of me wanted to rebel, to snap at him and tell him he didn't know what was going on. Zoe needed help right now, not to wait for my interrogation. Fortunately, the other part of me understood that fighting here was the fastest way to throw everything away. I opened my mouth to speak.

"He helped me get away," Zoe said.

"Hm?" Rehsman had never turned his gaze away from Zoe, but now he turned his attention back.

"He was on the street where it happened. He helped me get away from Kris Allens."

"Kris Allens, did all this?" There was dripping disappointment in Rehsman's voice. Something prickled under my skin. Something powerful.

I could stop time. Why was I letting them do this? I could freeze everything right now, and there would be nothing they could do to stop me. I could just take the knife and—

This was what Zoe'd been talking about. Fight or flight. That wasn't who I was. It was just a thought, almost like an unfamiliar voice in my head.

Zoe nodded after a moment, answering Rehsman's earlier question. "He found his soulmate."

Rehsman tsked. "They've already fled the scene, and my one

useful telepath is here on the ground." The man shook his head. His expression hadn't changed as he spoke. He wore discontent as a baseline. "Reg. Maddy. Get them cleaned up."

The burly man nodded.

"Debrief me when you're back, McCourtney." Before he finished speaking, Reshman took a step backward into the air, and another vermilion split formed. He disappeared into it.

There was a reason he was the coordinator of the DPR.

The man, Reg, came over to us, taking a knee in front of Zoe. She didn't look up at him, still staring glassy-eyed at the pier. "Fuck kid, they got you good, didn't they?"

Zoe didn't nod. I wasn't sure if she was lost in thought or just didn't have the strength anymore.

"It's okay," he said. The man got an arm under Zoe's shoulder and heaved her off the ground. He made it look easy.

I went to stand, but a hand pressed down on my shoulder, the sharp brunette. "I'm Officer Maddison Kingsmill. I'll escort you."

"I—"

"Officer McCourtney requires a specialized treatment facility," she said. Zoe was still mostly catatonic on Reg's shoulder, so she didn't protest. "I'll take you to a normal one. Quicker service."

"I just—" I started.

"Sir. She'll be fine. Thank you for your assistance in this matter, but this is in the hands of the Department of Power Regulation now."

"Maddy," Reg spoke up, "don't be all formal. He just helped save the kid."

Officer Kingsmill sighed behind me. "Fine. But we can't take him to the treatment center."

"We could," Reg said. "Just to make sure he's okay."

I was about to speak up to agree with Reg. That way, I could stay with Zoe and ensure she was okay, but I saw Zoe out of the corner of my eye.

She was shaking her head. Why?

"It's fine," I said after a moment, doing my best to hide the confusion in my voice. "I just want to go to the closest hospital. Everything hurts."

"Sounds good. Car will be here soon. We'll get you patched up before we get statements," Maddy said. She let go of my shoulder as she spoke, giving me one last chance to check on Zoe.

She was gone, nothing behind the eyes again. Breathing, but barely there. What had happened back there? We hadn't had time to talk about it.

I'd saved Zoe.

But what had I done?

13

Toby - Together

Fixed. Debriefed. Dismissed.

From what I could tell, the DPR was mostly trying to make this incident disappear. They didn't ask about the man who'd been stabbed in the street. They barely asked about Zoe. They just asked where I'd been that evening before the incident and then sent me home. No fanfare, nothing. Just told me to get back to civilian life.

Before, part of me wondered what happened to the people I'd seen on the news, what happened after the chaos and the trauma were over. It was only now that I realized I'd never cared enough to look into it. People didn't care what happened after the blood.

After the blood on my hands. The blood on Zoe's face.

Instead of rewashing my hands, I growled in frustration, throwing my phone toward the couch. I missed, and it landed screen down on the floor. I watched glittering glass scatter across the false hardwood. The screen had already cracked last night. Who gave a shit about it now?

Who gave a shit about any of this?

They'd told me to go back to a normal life, but there wasn't a normal life to go back to. Those people. That girl that'd killed Zoe. They'd been coming after me. Emma and I couldn't be together. Zoe was half-catatonic in the hospital. What the fuck kind of normal life was that?

Hell, until I'd managed a vague text message back, Todd had

thought I was dead or worse.

And I couldn't do anything about any of it. I could apparently stop time, and I was somehow worse than useless. For the first time, I was theoretically powerful, and all it had made me was the problem. Fucking years of wishing that I had something other than enhanced perception, and now...

What a joke.

I walked over and picked my phone up off the floor. A splinter of glass tumbled from the screen, followed by two more. What had been a spider web across my phone was now a shattered and useless mess. The LED display stuttered under the broken glass, flickering between black and every other color in the rainbow.

So much for getting back to Todd.

I took a deep breath. The air in the apartment was heavy and stifling, as if the walls were closing in. I wasn't allowed to reach out to anyone about what was going on. I couldn't search for anything about it online. I couldn't. I couldn't. I couldn't. People kept telling me what I couldn't do. Was I supposed to just sit here and wait, literally listening to the clock's second hand ticking by?

Pinpricks assaulted the inside of my skin again, the same pressure I'd felt on the pier. The pressure to flare up. The pressure to stop time and do something about my situation. I didn't know if it would change anything, but my power was presenting itself as a solution again. I just had to get angrier. I had to be more aggressive. I had to—

Zoe's thesis was on the coffee table. A Look Into the Fight or Flight Response in PSI Level Individuals. Maybe I needed to learn all the lingo so I could understand her research. It seemed like it was becoming pertinent.

I grabbed the spiral-bound paper off the table but paused halfway through righting myself. The clock wasn't ticking anymore.

Then a knock at the door.

I took a deep breath. There was only one person who could be waiting outside.

Emma was in the doorway when I opened it, dressed in quiet

clothes instead of the full business or business casual I'd seen her in thus far. She took half a step back as she saw me, almost like she hadn't expected me to be home.

Or maybe she'd just been rethinking this until I'd found her.

"Hey," I said, "nice to see you."

"I know I'm not supposed to be here," she said a little too quick, "but I heard about what happened and—"

"You heard?"

"Some of it," she corrected. "I was able to get a minute alone with Zoe, but they have her in the full treatment center, so there really isn't anywhere we could talk about any of..." She looked me over. "Well, any of this."

A treatment center sounded like it'd be nice. I'd had a doctor heal up my dislocated arm before they tossed me out of the emergency room. At least Officer Kingsmill had ensured that they served me quickly. "So you're here to ask?"

"No. Well. Yes," she sighed. "I didn't want to leave you alone through all of this and...Look, I know I shouldn't be here, and I figure as long as we talked about what's going on, then we'd at least have an excuse that wasn't just..."

"Empathy?" I suggested.

"When you put it like that, I feel like an asshole for needing an excuse," she sighed. "Mind if I come inside?"

"By all means. Your place, too."

"My place?"

"Figure it will be," I said. I stepped out of the way, and Emma paused at the door to, thankfully, take off her shoes. Her socks had tiny hearts on the heel, normally hidden from view. Cute. "You know, with the whole soulmates thing."

"Honestly, I hadn't thought about that part," she said. After a second, she dug around in her purse. "I brought the notepad, by the way, in case we wanted to add to our evidence folder." She produced the little yellow thing and tossed it toward the coffee table.

The notepad froze in midair.

"Oh."

"Yeah, it does that." I walked over and grabbed the notepad from stasis. The word soulmate had been circled several more times since I'd last seen it. After my glance, I put it down on the coffee table beside Zoe's dissertation. When I turned back to Emma, she stared at the spiral-bound papers. "Zoe lent it to me," I explained, "thought it would help."

Emma bit her lip. "Are you feeling that?" she asked.

I half-nodded, just enough to confirm without continuing the conversation. "Do you want coffee? Tea?" I headed over to the kitchen as I asked.

"Can you boil water when we're like this?"

I closed the cabinet I'd opened. "How about water?"

"I'm fine, thanks," Emma said.

Knowing that, I aborted the beverage mission and turned back to Emma. She was leaning back on the well-loved chair in the corner, sitting more on the armrest than the seat.

"What happened?" Emma asked.

"Last night?"

"Yeah."

"The girl I ran into outside the DPR when I was going to meet Zoe showed up at the bar. I followed her and some other people outside once I noticed they were acting strange." I saw Emma tense as I spoke, as if she knew how to correct my actions, but didn't want to speak up. "They said they wanted to talk. I tried to run. Todd got involved."

"Todd okay?"

"Yeah," I said. "He doesn't know what the fuck is going on, and he's worried, but he's okay. Not hurt, at least."

"And those people. Kris Allens was with them?" she asked.

"I don't know who that is."

"Dark skin. Reddish eyes. Short hair. Probably in a red coat."

"He wasn't there to start, but he was there when I went back for

Zoe."

Emma blinked twice. "Went back for Zoe?" She wouldn't have heard that in the debrief, and Zoe couldn't have explained that to her.

"Zoe, far as I can tell, lost the fight with the people who tried to grab me. She died..." I swallowed. "And then she didn't."

"You?"

"She was about to get executed when I ran back for her. I..." Another deep breath. I was skipping the worst part of this, wasn't I? I'd killed someone. Emma's soulmate was a killer and...

I watched Emma for half a second of quiet in the conversation. She was curled on the arm of the chair with her hair up in a messy bun right now, but she was a killer too, wasn't she? Or at least she'd signed off on it. I hadn't thought of it like that before.

"Toby?"

"Sorry. I froze time alone and ran back for her. Pulled her away from the Kris guy and brought her to the pier."

"That explains that," Emma nodded along.

"What?" I asked.

"I spoke to Reg when I visited Zoe for a minute. He said that eyewitnesses claimed she'd died on the scene but—"

"She did," I affirmed, "and she remembers it."

"What the fuck?" Emma said so quietly that she was practically mouthing it.

"Yeah," I said. I realized I'd been drumming my fingers on the counter, so I stopped.

"You saved her."

"I—"

"No, Toby." Emma stood up from her place on the armrest and crossed the distance between us. She rested her soft hand on my cheek before she continued speaking. "You saved Zoe. Don't... don't think about anything other than that. Okay?"

Oh. So she knew.

Emma bit her lip again as she caught my reaction. "I'm sorry,

Toby. The first time's hard. I know."

"Is it like a loyalty card? Every tenth is easier?" I forced the joke, and it barely made it out as one.

Emma looked around the room for a moment, but never took her hand off my cheek. It was dim in here. I'd never turned on the lights, but in our little paused reality the scattered bouncing sunlight from the window gave Emma a warm glow. "Doing what you have to do doesn't make you a worse person, Toby."

That was one way to avoid admitting whether she'd done it.

"I never thought I'd end up with someone like you and that you'd get caught up in this life," she sighed. "You know, it was supposed to be a blind date with someone who could use a break from their power. A little quiet in the middle of a city where they notice everything."

"Is that how Todd pitched me?"

"No, it's just how the picture goes in my head if you remove the stopping time part," she said.

"You imagine us not being soulmates?"

"Just that maybe you got super perception or something instead of this," she said. "I don't want to picture a world where I don't meet my soulmate in that bar."

"You saying you love me?" I asked.

"I'm saying I can see how we get there."

"Hey, we've had one date. That just means you think I'm hot."

"And?"

"I mean, I'll take it."

Emma let go of my cheek. "You saved Zoe too. That's gotta count for something. You get some points for that."

"Just points?"

Emma laughed. I hadn't heard a genuine laugh from her since the bar. It was beautiful, even if it was a little too dorky for her put-together aesthetic. "Maybe more later, but I don't think it's the time."

"We have no idea what time it is," I pointed out.

"It's been like five minutes. You know exactly what time it is."

"Three twenty-four," I said, "give or take a few skipped heartbeats."

"Okay." Emma poked me in the sternum and walked away. "Now you're laying it on too thick."

"Romance is a pleasant distraction," I said.

Emma chuckled again, but didn't come back. I felt my shoulders slump an inch before the disappointment hit. "Speaking of distractions," Emma said. "Do you wanna know what's complete bullshit?"

"What?"

"We've been so focused on this that I don't know how you affect me," she said. "You spend your life thinking about your soulmate and what they'd do to your power, and now I don't get to know. "

I nodded, even though I'd never given that part much thought.

"You're obviously immune to me, which makes sense, but that just means I can't see how I work on other people."

"How do you know I'm immune?" I asked.

Emma pointed at the clock, but I shook my head.

"Have you tried turning me off?" I asked.

"No, and I haven't tried to turn you on either."

"Really?"

"You'd know if I was trying."

"Noted." I nodded along and marked it down as something to look forward to. "But actually. You haven't tried to turn my power off yet."

"Not how I work, Toby," Emma said. "I'm like you. It just works. If I could be selective about who I affected, I'd have lived a very different life."

"And?" I asked. I waved to myself, telling her to try.

"It's not how it works."

"I stop time when I'm around you, Emma," I pointed out. "Do it for the notepad."

"For the notepad?"

"We've added nothing to it today."

"Fine," Emma only half said the word as it melded into an exasperated sigh. She pointed a finger at me. "Off."

I waited for a second, but the second hand didn't tick.

"See?" she said.

"That's not trying."

"That's—"

"I am new to this power-science thing. Just give my idea a real shot."

Emma opened her mouth to protest and then took a deep breath instead. I couldn't tell if it was to prepare or to summon the patience to deal with my insistence. Emma held out her hand this time, pointing her entire palm toward me.

After a second, I shook my head. Emma didn't move.

A bead of sweat formed on her forehead. Emma shut her eyes.

Across the room, the second hand stuttered back to life.

14
Zoe - The Call

The mental stress on subjects with high-level abilities over time has been thoroughly documented and is covered within the attached references. This stress has been taken into consideration in regard to the results and expectations of the following experiments. All subjects within this study have been exposed to the stress effects and Upsilon-Psi level abilities for a minimum of 20 years. Any subject with different circumstances will be noted but not included in the results of this...

I flipped further into the study, feeling the crisp pages slip between my fingers as I did. I'd read this at least a dozen times, but I'd just wanted something familiar. Something that would help me relax.

It didn't help that I was painfully aware that I was trying to relax. Relaxing was like sleeping. I just had to accept it and let it happen, but I'd never been good at either. I could head the seconds ticking by in my head, painfully slow, each one dragging its feet before clicking over to the next.

So I kept reading.

Subject: Zoe McCourtney

Test One: Stress testing.

I skipped down the page.

After extensive testing, McCourtney's abilities assumed control of most of her functions, performing high-level tasks while the subject was only partially conscious and unaware of their surroundings. McCourtney lost fine control over most actions during this time, leaving her unable to adjust the kinetic force applied by her power. 58% of the way into the experiment, a spike in her abilities allowed her to disable and damage our equipment while she was locked in the testing chamber.

McCourtney did not have a line of sight, nor a direct pathway to our equipment from the other room. This ability to affect objects that the subject is unaware of is unprecedented within studied Telekinetic Abilities, as well as the abilities she displayed during initial testing where the subject remained conscious.

The book slammed shut and almost caught my fingers. I swore and looked over to the door to see if anyone was coming in. Either the man they'd stationed outside didn't care, or he hadn't heard me. It didn't really matter which.

I pushed myself out of the chair and stumbled forward. The power was staggered, uneven. In the past hours, I'd regained some mobility, but it wasn't enough. It was shoddy, inconsistent work.

I let the book tumble to the floor. Reading wasn't helping, and I didn't know what else I could do. I'd been taken to a healer as soon as they'd found me and Toby, but nothing was the same. Even worse, they'd put me on fucking house arrest to ensure I recovered. I knew it was a cover-up. They could tell something was wrong with me when they'd patched me up. They just didn't know what it was.

Not that I did either.

I wrapped my power around the book on the floor, and it complied, but that was all it did. My mental coils held tight around the book, waiting for another command, for another exacting explanation of what they had to do. Where was the control? Where was the unconscious collaboration? I didn't need to tell my arm to bend at the elbow, and my power had always felt the same, barely a thought and it would do what I wanted.

Hell, half the time I'd never had to think at all.

A twinge of pain shot up my cheek, and the book caved in on itself. I swore again before shooting my hand up. My cheek was fine.

The skin was smooth and cool save for a bandage where I'd clawed my skin raw from incessant scratching. It wasn't melted and burned. It wasn't...

That hadn't happened.

That had never happened.

None of it was real anymore.

The ballpoint pen on the table jumped, but then all it did was spin in place. They'd told me to write about what'd happened that day, both for my mental health and because they didn't understand it. As far as they knew, I'd never died. As far as they knew, I'd just gotten my ass kicked. Eyewitnesses said that they'd seen me torched on the pavement, and I'd felt the fire melting my skin, but—

I had broken legs I could walk on. I had clean skin that had burned away. I was alive after being dead.

Toby.

My hand twitched, and my power slapped it before I could. I took a deep breath.

I grabbed the pen from its spinning spot over the counter. It felt like a foreign object in my fingers. How long had it been since I'd handwritten something? I pressed the pen down onto the pad of paper they'd given me, but all I did was slowly stain it with ink.

I wrote about nothing. My words were barely recognizable. A series of scratches on the paper, marks to show that I was still here. A step below idle thoughts. My power flicked the lights on and off in the background, cycling the room as the seconds ticked by.

By the time I was done, I'd coated the white paper in blue ink.

Once I was out of here, I had to see Toby. I had to run him through every test we had. We had to understand his power. I needed to understand his power. I had to know what happened to me. We needed answers before people started asking questions. I could fill out the damage reports and make up a cover story, but how long would that buy us? How many excuses did I have in me? How long did we have before they were back?

I should have crushed everyone there last night. Kris had taken me by surprise with his new bitch, but I was the strongest person in this damned city. Hell, I was the strongest person on the continent. If I hadn't been distracted, if I hadn't been focused on something else, I would have...

Fuck.

My power picked up the pen again and idly dragged it back and forth on the paper, scoring a line down the middle, sawing through the first sheet, then setting to work on the second. It wasn't productive, but it was something.

I took a deep breath and tried to focus on single letters. Words. Something that I could use as an anchor for my mind to keep it in one place long enough to—

The pen continued to carve back and forth on the sheet. The lights flicked on and off again.

Another deep breath. I could figure this out. I was in control. I was in charge.

The lights again.

I needed to calm down. I had to stop thinking about how I'd been on the ground. How I'd been burned. How I'd—

The lights.

I was alive. I'd be on watch for a day or two, and then I'd be out. I'd be—

The. Fucking. Lights.

The room shook as I raised a hand, tearing the switch out of the wall and the fixture out of the ceiling. Drywall cracked and splintered. Dust showered through the room. A tangled mess of wires and shattered glass crumpled at my feet. The glass shone in the middling daylight in the now-dark apartment.

I closed my eyes in the waning daylight of the apartment. Most days, I could have felt the dust falling around me. I could have counted the splinters of drywall scattered across the living room. I could have measured the twisted and torn wires I'd left strewn across the floor.

Today, I felt nothing. I just heard thoughts. The entirety of Crescent chattering incessantly, melding into a solid static that always dragged at my attention. Pulled at my—

The door opened.

"Zoe?"

Steve was the man assigned to 'guard' me, which was laughable considering the gap between us. The department just wanted someone at the door watching me and—

"What the fuck just happened in here?" he asked.

"Steve."

"Zoe, is everything—"

"I'm. Fine." My power pressed on the door to close it, but Steve held it in place. How weak was I right now?

"Do you need anything? It..." Steve trailed off, but I could hear his thoughts.

How can I say this in a way that won't piss her off?

"Just looks like you're having a rough day," he said.

"Just space."

"Zoe."

"Space," I hissed. This time, I slammed the door on him, and I felt the hinges shake.

Steve tried the handle again.

"Space, Steve," I said, even though he couldn't hear me. Fuck. I was a mess. Now he was going to call that in, and they were going to keep me on watch for what? Weeks? Months? We didn't have that sort of time. I needed to be back out there so I could help Emma, so I could help Toby.

So I could hunt down the people that killed me.

For the first time since I'd woken up by the docks, I felt the surrounding room. I felt the spark of united purpose in my head that kept me in control.

I took a deep breath, and everything in the room that wasn't bolted down floated several inches off the ground. It all waited until I breathed out to land.

Was that the key? Maybe I just had to—

Outside the door, Steve stumbled as he landed.

"Steve," I called, just loud enough that he could hear it. "I can feel you outside."

"Sorry, Zoe!"

Where was I? Right. Maybe I just had to find the people that killed me and get rid of them. Once I'd done that, I'd be able to think again. I'd be in control again. I'd be safe. Emma and Toby would be safe. It was—

Steve took a step outside the door.

I didn't have my phone, but I could at least email Emma and let her know what—

Steve put his hand in his pocket.

"Fucking—" I snapped, but my words weren't fast enough. Before I understood the motion, my hand had shot toward the door, and a wave of force followed. Drywall, wood, steel, and bone shattered and scattered in a concussive blast, shooting out as I demolished the side of the building and vaporized everything in its path.

Drywall dust, drops of water, and red mist hung in the air where there'd used to be a hallway and—

"Oh God."

I tried to stumble backward, but I was already floating several inches off the ground, my power wreathed around me, holding me sure and steady.

What had I just done?

What was I about to do?

I could feel my hands trying to shake, but my mind wouldn't let them, locking them in perfect place and posture.

There was only one thing I could do at this point. I had to make this better. I was going to fix this. I'd hunt them down. That thought had been the only thing keeping me in control. I'd kill them.

One bastard at a time.

15

Zoe - One Woman War

By the time the sirens reached my old condo, they were on the wrong side of the city. I'd always felt so scared before. Scared of what breaking the sound barrier would do. Of who I could hurt. But right now? Right now, they could take it. There were more important things than a couple ear drums scattered across the city.

As soon as I'd gotten out of the apartment, I'd been able to think. I could hear all the voices in Crescent at once... That meant I could find anyone.

The sign age and streets of Crescent flashed past below me. It all felt so easy now. What had I been so afraid of? I was so powerful. I should have been doing this years ago.

I slammed down into the courtyard of the Hammond Luxury Suites, a worn-down piece of shit apartment complex on the wrong side of town. The buildings were a sad robin-egg blue that had faded and streaked over time. Any windows on the bottom floors were either barred or broken. Frankly, it was the kind of place where my uniform would have caused people to scatter. I wasn't wearing my uniform today, but I had something different.

Fucking power.

A cool breeze ran through the afternoon carrying the salt of the ocean choked by city smog; it washed over me as I closed my eyes. I'd been able to track them to this complex, but back at my place, it had been too far to find out which unit. Now that I was in the courtyard?

I walked to the center of the complex, standing beside an old fountain that was a remnant of this place's aspirational origins. Now it was a monument to its decay, cracked, covered in graffiti, and it hadn't held water in the better part of a decade.

Usually, coming this close to find someone came with the risk of them seeing me in advance, but who cared if she saw me first? I was looking for a fight.

I scanned the thoughts of the complex. Money troubles. Complaints about the noise I'd just made. Too many eyes tuned into the beginning of Gladius season. Then I found the name.

Without a prompt, my power snapped the top off of the shitty courtyard fountain. Before the first pebbles settled, the rubble shot off like a bullet, crashing into the fifteenth floor, smashing balcony and plaster where the window would have worked.

There were the first screams. I shook my head to try to quiet the thoughts that got louder with them. They just had to let me work. There were rats in this nest.

The dust drifted down like snow, and plaster cracked in the hole I'd made, but no heads followed it. Nobody in there was brave enough to come down here and fight me. Which meant I needed to go to them.

I was at the balcony's edge faster than my fountain piece had been. The wind whipped after me, blowing drywall dust into the apartment and coating the three standing occupants as they stared back at me. There were two I didn't recognize, but Lexi was bent over and trying to help a woman stagger to her feet. I waited in the blasted hole for her to clock me.

"You? But you're—"

"Didn't take," I hissed. Behind me, the metal balcony railing twisted and sheared into pieces, each falling into formation behind me as they tore free.

The two still standing in the room that weren't Lexi steadied themselves, the woman raising her hands and the man taking a deep breath. Lexi looked over to them. I saw her barrier slither over her skin, wrapping her in a ghostly second layer.

Coward.

"We surrender," Lexi said.

What?

"We surrender. Okay? We'll come quietly, just don't…" she trailed off as she read my expression.

She couldn't just do that. She didn't get to do that. She didn't get to kill me and then give up. That wasn't how this worked. I was getting my rematch.

Lexi's eyes widened. "Run!"

The woman turned first, but I waved a hand in her direction. My power wrapped around her throat and yanked her toward me. I half-stepped out of the way, and she careened off the balcony, screaming. Her cry echoed through the courtyard before cutting off abruptly. One down.

The man tried to yell her name, but I stopped him short. A curt nod sent the metal shards behind me flying, each skewering and pinning him to the wall. He gagged as each one stabbed into his skin while the collective avoided a killing blow.

Lexi was still trying to pull the injured woman off the floor.

"Where's the girl from yesterday?" I asked. "Where's the confidence? The shit-talking?"

"You crazy bitch."

"I'm the crazy bitch?" I cackled at that as my hand drifted up to the bandage on my cheek. "You fucking killed me. Out in the street. You left me to die, and you're going to call me—"

"How are you not dead?!" she screamed. She tried one more time to heave up the woman on the floor, but couldn't manage it. Lexi put herself between me and the girl, raising a barrier between us.

The man pinned to the wall gagged.

"You killed me," I repeated. "Don't try to hide now."

Lexi glanced to the side, but there wasn't an exit, and it didn't look like she was leaving the woman behind.

"You want to run?" I asked. "You were so brave with Kris around. What happened?" I raised a hand. The apartment shook under our feet. "What was it you said?" I asked.

"I don't know you—"

"Ain't soulmates a bitch," I spat, "and you're right, because he's not close enough to save you now."

Lexi looked down at the woman again. I pulled the apartment out from under her, tearing the floor below us out of the building and throwing it toward the courtyard.

Dust, water, and paper sprayed. The injured woman screamed. Lexi was in freefall.

She didn't get off that easy.

I summoned another wave of force and called it across the courtyard, building it foot by foot until it batted Lexi out of mid-air, slamming her back into the building she'd been falling away from. She disappeared through the drywall and slammed into the steel bars between apartments.

Outside, the apartment I'd torn from the building crashed to the ground, smashing into the cobblestone and splintering across the courtyard. Desks, drywall, porcelain, and blood mixed in the rubble; all three distractions' tangled bodies were wrapped around steel and plaster.

Dust dripped from the ceiling as I stared down at the disaster scene. I heard something crack in the apartment above. There were more screams, this time from the collateral damage.

I'd given them enough time to leave. I had work to do.

The sound of breaking glass and splintering wood echoed off the bleak courtyard walls, but I kept my attention on the Lexi-shaped hole I'd made in the hallway beyond. I couldn't feel her, I never could when she had the barrier up, but we were on the fifteenth floor. Where was she going to run? What was she going to do?

I couldn't feel Lexi. I never could when she had the barrier up, but we were on the fifteenth floor. Where was she going to run? What was she going to do?

I floated from the empty spot where the apartment had been

and landed in the hallway beyond. I could feel my hair and hood blowing in the wind instead of getting held in perfect place. It was strange, but I didn't need aesthetics right now. I needed firepower.

Lexi was still crumpled against the wall, having left a crater where she hit and slammed into the metal. I could see that her eyes were open. She wasn't unconscious. She was just a coward. "Get up," I said.

Lexi didn't answer.

"You fucking killed me," I snapped. It almost didn't sound like me, like something was broken behind my vocal cords. "I said get up."

She was still silent.

"You don't get to do this," I hissed. I leaned down to her. If she didn't have the damn shield, I would have grabbed her by the damned ponytail myself.

"We surrendered," she said, "and you killed them."

"Fuck off." My power wrapped around her, coiling tighter than I'd managed last night. I kept my hold on her even as her shields tried to force me off. I pulled her up to my face. At first, her eyes were downcast, and then she looked up.

I saw the spark behind her eyes. Maybe there was some fight left in her after all. Not that it mattered at this point. Four down. Countless to go.

"Fine, you're coming with me," I said after I'd held her in place for a moment.

"Really?" she asked. The spark in her eyes manifested as hope in her voice.

"No." My power snapped Lexi backward, throwing her back through the apartment building and out into the open air above the courtyard. She screamed. I heard her cry the bastard's name. "Call it insurance," I said. I waited to hear her crack against the ground, but the approaching sirens drowned out my satisfaction.

I flew out of the building and down into the courtyard, landing further than Lexi would have fallen. People were pointing at me and staring at the rubble. I wanted them gone. I wanted to be here alone so I could see that Lexi was dead. That I'd done it right. That it was finished.

The sirens. I heard a voice behind me.

"Target in sight. Engaging."

The surrounding cobblestones cracked under the weight of my power. I had to find Lexi. She wouldn't have died in that fall. I had to —

"Ma'am, I'm Field Officer Reginald Forte from the Department of Power Regulation. What's going…" He trailed off as I turned. "Kid?"

Broken plates and wooden beams from the shattered apartment on the ground wrested themselves from the rubble as I raised a hand toward him.

"Kid. What are you doing? What the hell is—" His eyes darted around, trying to mark everything my power had picked up in the last seconds. "Don't do this." He got low. "Don't make me do this, Zoe."

I blinked, and my power retreated for a breath.

Reg stomped the ground. The earth shot up from my feet and swallowed me.

16

Toby - A Race Against

There were cars on the road. There were speeders on the side of the road. And then there was Emma.

An old-school gasoline engine roared under us as we shot down the street. We were together for the first time since we'd met, and Emma was taking me on a ride. She'd never been able to drive cars that depended on charge powers, which meant she'd been locked to older models. That it was a fierce motorcycle? That was just personal preference.

The road beneath us was a mix of smooth asphalt and cracked pavement, occasionally littered with stray debris that Emma dodged with ease. The dead-gray office buildings of the core flashed by on either side, barely recognizable with how fast Emma kept us moving.

Emma dropped a gear to accelerate and pass a black truck, skirting along the outside of the lane to squeeze past. I held my breath. There were inches between us and the car. I could tell that we weren't going to crash, even at this speed, but with Emma's normal perception, she couldn't have known. It was all raw feel and intuition.

Objectively terrifying.

A moment later, Emma pulled to a stop as a light changed. We'd been heading back to her condo to tell Zoe what we'd figured out, but at this point, it was clear that Emma was taking the long way home. Once we were in park, Emma spoke up, her voice barely muffled by the helmet. "You doing okay back there?"

"Great." It was half the truth. Part of me was doing great.

"You look a little windswept."

"It's windy back here."

"Fast enough?" she asked.

I held up a weak thumbs up.

Emma didn't offer a verbal response. She just laughed and tapped her heel on the side of the bike, counting the seconds on the crossing sign to our right.

The past hour had been pleasant, almost like we were back at the bar when she'd had a little liquid courage to make our situation less terrifying. Now Emma had to find other ways to make our relationship dangerous.

I took a deep breath in preparation for Emma shooting off the line, but it never happened. Instead, Emma let the bike rest to the side and spoke, though it was barely audible over the helmet. "Go for Terish." I couldn't hear the person on the other end of the call, but I listened to the squeaking leather of Emma's gloves as she tightened her grip on the handlebars.

The truck we'd flown past drove by. The driver flipped us off. Honestly fair. I kind of agreed with him.

"What the fuck do you mean, she's under—Yeah, go ahead." Emma bristled at the last part. I pressed closer against her back. She was warm, but more importantly, I was trying to understand the conversation. No matter how close I got, not even I could catch what the other side was saying. "Fuck, fuck, fuck," she continued.

"Emma?" I asked. She held up a finger in response.

I rolled my eyes. Not that she'd turned around to see my display. "On my way," she said. Then, after a second, presumably after hanging up. "Fucking shit." She kicked the side of her bike hard enough that I glanced at the paint job to see how it was holding up.

"What's going on?" I asked.

"Know how I told you that Zoe's under house arrest for a day or two?" she asked.

"Yeah."

"Not anymore." Emma revved the engine. "She broke out of the house and tried to hunt some of the Red that attacked you guys last night down."

"Is she okay?" It felt like a dumb question considering what I knew about Zoe, but last time...

"I don't have all the details, but there are fucking casualties, Toby." Emma checked over her shoulder to ensure we had time to kick off the sidewalk. "What the hell are you doing?" Emma asked, and I knew it wasn't about me.

The first raindrops of a fall storm splattered against the pavement, staining it dark.

I took a deep breath.

Emma kicked off the sidewalk and flipped on the sirens and lights on the front of her bike. In a terrifying moment, I realized she hadn't been going fast before; she'd been taking it easy on me. We screamed down the street, whipping past the black truck for the second time.

The buildings on either side of us melded into a blur. I could feel the engine straining under our speed, but the lights in front of us just continued manifesting green, daring Emma to go faster, to push harder to—

I was holding onto her as a seatbelt, but I turned at least part of that into trying to support her. Her back muscles softened at my touch, but she didn't slow down. She couldn't.

For the second time in the past few days, I was outside the DPR head office, staring down its foreboding but quiet exterior. It's incredible how quickly life changes.

Emma pulled off her helmet before we'd fully come to a stop, and she knocked the kickstand open with her foot. "Toby, you're staying here with the bike."

"What?" I asked. "I can help."

"I don't want to get you involved in there, and based on what I heard, no yo—"

The air across the street split open, a brilliant vermilion crack forming before Callum Rehsman walked out into the street and approached. Emma pushed for me to get off the motorcycle. I complied.

"About time, Emma," Rehsman said before turning his attention to me, "and I didn't think I would meet you again. Toby, right?"

"Yeah," I answered. Emma handed her helmet to me and began pulling her hair back up.

"First on the scene with Ms. McCourtney, and now riding around with another one of my agents." Rehsman's voice was almost too still, like there had never been an emotion behind it. "You're just everywhere, aren't you, Mr. Vander?"

My blood chilled at that. If Emma was worried about him knowing me, she didn't show it.

"Where's Zoe?" Emma asked. She was took off her gloves as she spoke. I reached out to grab them for her as well. "Is she in a cell?"

Rehsman glanced at me in response to Emma's question. "A touch comfortable around the civilians, Director Tavish."

"He knows who she is," Emma said. "Now let me see her."

"Certainly. You know where lower containment is."

Emma walked toward the building and then stopped when Rehsman didn't join her. "Sir?"

"Oh, I don't believe I'll be useful for this part," Rehsman said. "McCourtney has always bristled against my authority."

Emma paused for almost too long. "I'll report once we have information, sir." Once she'd nodded to him, Emma waited for a second. Rehsman turned back to me. Emma swallowed spit, then nodded in my direction.

I did my best to look like I wasn't watching her, but I kept an eye until she disappeared through the front doors.

Despite the traffic we'd weaved through on the way here, the street was almost silent in front of the DPR. It was just me and Callum Rehsman, who was taking the opportunity to examine each and every detail about me.

Finally, after what felt like an eternity, he spoke up. "Are you feeling alright after your last adventure? Officer Kingsmill took good care of you?"

I hadn't realized I was holding my breath, but I exhaled at the question. "Physically feeling better."

"Mentally?" he asked. There was no body language to read on the man. He was either perfectly trained, or I didn't want to know what happened in his head. "The trauma associated with events like those last night shouldn't be overlooked."

"Been better," I said. I was trying to stick as close to the truth as I could. It was always easier to lie that way. I should have been a better liar than I was, considering I knew most of the tells, but I'd never gotten the hang of it. "Harrowing."

"The DPR thanks you for your service. As you can imagine, Field Officer McCourtney is a critical asset to our arsenal and our team here in Crescent." Rehsman offered a hand. I accepted. It was mechanical, insincere. "But I have to ask," he began, his grip tightened as he spoke, "I had multiple eyewitnesses who claimed to see Ms. McCourtney die on the scene. I read over your file, and it said your power was—"

"Enhanced perception."

Rehsman's grip eased. "Suppose you just saw better than everyone else there then? Figured out she was injured instead of dead."

"Sounds about right." I took the chance to put Emma's helmet and gloves down on the bike instead of meeting Rehsman's gaze as I said that. Hopefully, it would keep him from digging deeper.

Or, more accurately, seeing a reason to do so.

"Well, as I said, the DPR thanks you for what you did with Officer McCourtney. If Director Tavish hasn't been clear about that, I hope I have."

"I appreciate it."

"Now, Mr. Vander." Rehsman looked down the street at an oncoming car, waiting for it to pass. He was perfectly centered on the DPR office behind him, as if he were part of the looming architecture. "The reason I wanted to speak to you out here is because I wanted to caution you about something..."

"Okay."

"The man Officer McCourtney mentioned last night, Kris Allens. He belongs to, in fact, he leads, a regiment of terrorists against power regulation."

"Against the DPR?"

"The concept as a whole, Mr. Vander," Rehsman corrected, "people like Mr. Allens are dangerous. I would suggest you use caution in the coming days considering, as I understand it, you're the one who rescued Officer McCourtney, and Kris Allens would have been desperate to kill her himself."

"Thank you."

"Unfortunately, the debate over power regulation sometimes turns violent due to the actions of the powerful few. That's why we're here, Mr. Vander." Rehsman nodded. "The DPR keeps the average layman like yourself safe. Even if some people might disagree with the required methods." Rehsman let the last part linger, testing my reaction to it.

I tried not to feed him one.

A few moments later, after the test, he continued, "Stay safe. People with abilities like yours shouldn't get involved in this sort of thing. What was it again?" he asked. I knew he hadn't forgotten.

"Advanced perception."

"Right. Well, if you happen to have any questions about the characters you ran into last evening, I will be sure to let Director Tavish know she can speak to you with a level of moderate clearance about the subject. After all, once you've been exposed to the conflict, you start forming opinions."

"I think I just want to stay away from it," I said.

Rehsman chuckled; it was just as mechanical as his handshake had been. "You're a smart man, but not everyone has the option, Mr. Vander. That said, based on your power, I believe you might be able to slip under everyone's radar and live a quiet life after all." Rehsman nodded once, and then a vermilion portal opened in the air. For the first time I'd seen, he held it in place instead of walking or sending someone immediately through. "I'm sure Director Tavish will keep you on the right path if you need opinions. She has some to lend."

I nodded instead of offering words, but then spoke up in the last seconds before he disappeared. "Are you going inside to speak to them?" I asked.

"No. McCourtney bristles against me, as I mentioned. I'll be far away while our agents handle this today, Mr. Vander. Though..." Rehsman turned around and held out his hand. When I matched, he dropped a key into my palm. "You may have forgotten something in Ms. McCourtney's office during your last visit. Considering everything going on, you might want to grab it before someone else does."

My eyes widened. And Rehsman certainly caught it. The blood.

"That key is a debt repaid. Thank you again for securing Officer McCourtney. I'm sure we'll be in touch."

17

Zoe - Wrath of God

There was nothing, and then there was darkness and pressure. Had I been here before? Had I—

No. That had been something else. I was barely there, but I could think. That was more than there had been after the fight with Kris. I couldn't feel my body, but maybe... I tried to reach out with my power, and nothing answered on the other side.

I heard voices, muffled, but still clear enough to hear in the crushing silence I was trapped in.

"We're lowering the sedative dose now. She should be awake soon."

I tried to place the voice, and the only thing that came to mind was swirling dizziness. My brain's way of rejecting me while it was drunk on... they'd said a sedative.

I would have been trying to move, but I still couldn't feel my body.

A second voice. "That's everything you know? There has to be more to it." That one I recognized even when I could only access the top of my mind. Emma. That was Emma. She was here for me. Thank God.

I opened my mouth to say her name, but the command still didn't reach my muscles. At least I remembered I had a mouth.

"There's not," the first voice said. "I don't know what's going on. I found her like that. Like she'd—" The man cut himself off.

"Heartbeat is rising. She's stirring."

Like what? How had he found me? Where was I? I didn't want to be here. Last time, I didn't know where I was, I'd been dead. Was that what was happening? If I could, I would have shaken my head. No. I'd thought through that already. If I could think, that meant I was alive.

"That means I'm up, doesn't it?" Emma asked.

"I'll keep an eye from right outside the door, okay?"

"I'll be fine, it's Zoe."

"Emma."

"Reg, it's Zoe." The way she said my name was confident. Thank God she was here to set everything straight and get me out of whatever this was. "I'll be fine."

"Respectfully, Emma—"

"Out."

"Emma—"

"I'm not asking Reg. I'm ordering. Wait outside. She'll be awake, and I want a moment to talk to her alone."

"I... Yes, Emma. I'll be a yell away."

"Thank you," Emma said.

I could hear other things in the room now, beyond the voices. The rhythmic beep of a monitor and the heavy breathing of the machine behind it. The door on the far side of the room opened and closed.

My mind couldn't trace out the space I was in. Where was I?

The sound of a chair scraping across the ground, approaching.

Then Emma, "Oh Zoe." Her voice was dragging, heartbroken.

The words were enough to stir me. Knowing that I was part of the conversation forced my head to contain its thoughts and channel them into being awake as opposed to present. I tried to take a deep breath, but I wasn't controlling my breathing. The machine was.

I felt the tubes up my nose, feeding oxygen in despite my... How was I trapped? Did it matter? I tried to pull on the tubes with my mind, but the force slipped against the plastic, dripping off to the side. Of course. Emma was in the room. What else did I expect?

"Zo," Emma said. The back of her hand pressing against my forehead helped orient me, snapping my consciousness into my body with the first pinpricks of feeling. I was still numb. I didn't have limbs, but I at least understood that I was physically there.

I tried to open my mouth to speak; it was still too early for that. Even if I could feel my mouth, my tongue would be too heavy to lift.

I felt Emma leaning in, the slight breeze of her getting close. She was wearing perfume. "Take your time, Zoe. They wanted me to come here and talk to you and... I wanted to talk to you about what happened. About what's going on and... I suppose some of it should wait until you're awake."

Where were my fingers? If I could move them, then maybe I could start trying to get free and—

"Reg? Can we get the dose lowered again? I don't think she's gonna wake up like this."

I heard the door open.

"She's awake now," Reg said.

"I can't talk to her like this."

"Emma, you weren't there and—"

"Reg. I'm in the room. Even if she tried something, I'm sitting right beside her. There isn't anything she could do."

For the first time since waking up, I felt my power flare, pushing against the statement she'd just made by wreathing around my fingers—there they were— and pushing outward against the walls around me. I'd show her. I'd show her useless and—

What was I saying? That was Emma. She didn't think I was useless. She was just trying to help. I would never.

I felt awareness rush back as the door closed behind Reg, and he lowered the dosage of whatever they were pumping into me. In the first second, I was back; my power slithered along my arm, determining how much space there was between me and my cage. I was—

That was right. Reg had been the one that trapped me. I was wrapped in a ball of concrete. I'd seen it before, but I was always on the other end. I'd sat in the room while they conducted interviews to ensure the subject was telling the truth.

Now I was trapped in concrete in one of the containment rooms.

My mind didn't have the strength it needed to fight against the bonds, not with Emma sitting right across from me, but it could still move. It found the needle in my arm, the one pumping its poison into my system. I had to be awake if I wanted to explain myself to Emma. My power pulled, and the needle came loose. I felt the constant IV drip of their sedative wasting against my skin.

"There we go," Emma said after a few seconds without the sedative. "Good morning."

I tried to speak again, but my tongue was too heavy. I could at least find my eyelids, blinking away the darkness and looking at Emma for the first time.

She was windswept and disheveled. The first thing she offered was a smile, but I could see the worry behind it.

"Are you feeling okay, Zoe?" I didn't know if she understood that I couldn't respond yet. That I couldn't—

Of course, she knew. She understood. Emma was just giving me the time I needed to join the conversation. She was garnering sympathy from the people outside. Obviously, she knew me better than anyone. It was Emma. She must have known exactly what was going on. What I'd had to do. Why I'd done it. Everything.

She was everything I had. The only piece in the puzzle. The only person I could trust.

"Don't worry, Zoe," Emma said. I felt her hand against my torn cheek, the edge of her palm resting on the fresh bandages. "We're gonna get through this, okay?"

I tried to brush her away as reassurance, but I was trapped, and my mind wasn't clear enough to manifest around her hand. All I could do was wait.

Then I managed my first sound, barely a mumble, but it was something.

"There we go." I'd heard that tone before, back when she'd first started taking care of me as a pre-teen, "I just need you to tell me what's going on."

No, I was wrong. I hadn't heard that tone before. Something was different in the mix, but I couldn't place it. Fear? Apprehension? Hate?

No. It couldn't be any of those. This was Emma. It was Emma.

Pins and needles started in my chest and spread across my skin, prodding each nerve as my feeling came back. As soon as they'd moved past my ribs, I felt the pressure on my lungs, how tight I'd been wrapped in concrete and stone. How hard they'd tried to hold me down.

"Zoe," she said my name slowly, like she would hurt me with it.

"Emma," I coughed through my prison. Dull pain echoed through the sedatives. They'd definitely cracked my ribs again by throwing me in here.

"You feeling all right?" she asked. I took a second to notice the clipboard that was on her lap.

"Been better," I managed. "Get me out of this—" I tried to struggle, but I didn't have enough feeling to.

"What happened?"

"Let me out and—"

"Are you feeling better?" she asked. She was dodging my request. Why was she letting me stay like this? They'd thrown me in a cell, and she was just going along with it?

"Let me out."

"No," she finally acknowledged, "they won't let me do that until you talk to me."

"And you're siding with them?" The receding sedative and the fact that she was pissing me off combined to allow full sentences and thoughts.

"Yes, Zoe."

"Fuck you," I spat. "Why the hell—"

"I'm protecting you," Emma cut me off. "What the fuck do you think they want to do? You—"

"I need you to let me go because I'm not done."

"What do you mean, you're not done?"

"I need to go out there and hunt them—"

"No, Zoe, you don't. You're hurt. You're done."

"They're still out there."

"Fuck them. What the hell are you thinking, Zoe? You can't just go out on a rampage to—"

"I was trying to protect Toby."

Emma glanced at the door as I said the name. "You can't. He's safe. We need to protect you right now."

"From what?" I asked. "I just killed the bitch and three more for good measure. We've let them stay in the background for too long. If you just let me go, I can finish this and—"

"Thirty-two," Emma said.

"What?"

"Thirty-two people, Zoe. Not four. Thirty-two."

"What are you talking about?"

"At the apartments," Emma said. "You broke down half the North Tower. Did you not know what you were doing?"

"I knew exactly what I was doing," I spat. "Why are you on their side?"

"Thirty-two people, Zoe,"—Emma leaned in, almost too close—"You haven't heard what they're saying upstairs." She took a deep breath. "I'm here to protect you."

"Protect me from who? Nobody here can hurt me."

Emma sat back up. "I can, Zoe."

"Was that a threat?" I felt my power flare momentarily and found cracks in the concrete. My mind slithered into the spaces between stones and pushed, testing the limit, finding how much strength I could summon with Emma in my face.

"Of course not, but you're not invincible, and I don't know how, but you're still hurt."

"Trust me, I've never felt better than when I was out there and

—"

"I know you," she cut me off again. Why wasn't she letting me explain myself? "You're not like this. You wouldn't do that. Something is wrong, and we just need to figure out what—"

"I'm fine," I snapped. Emma's chair shook as I spoke, and her eyes widened. Maybe she was getting it now. "Why are you against me here?"

Emma closed her eyes and took a deep breath, then a second. I gave her space. My power was busy. It widened the gaps in the concrete prison, sawing them open millimeter by millimeter, breaking me out.

Emma finally spoke and did it wearing a soft, apprehensive smile. It looked like every other caring look she'd given me, but now I understood it for what it was. Manipulation. Emma was on their side. Why was she against me after all these years? We'd planned to run away together, and now—

I didn't hear Emma's words, but knew what I had to do. If I killed them all, it would prove me right. I could win her back. I could keep Toby safe. I could do anything.

My power flared at the thought, pushing beyond the bounds of Emma's presence. It knew what I needed to do. It was guiding me in the right direction. After all, my power came from my mind. How could it have been steering me wrong?

"Zoe," Emma raised her voice, snapping my attention back to her. She must have not wanted me to escape, she must have not wanted me to— "Zoe, are you okay? What's going on?"

Emma looked down as my power pushed out into the room, and her chair vibrated. "Zoe," she repeated, her voice cautious and scared.

She should have been, but I was going to pay her back for the years of goodwill with a final gift.

I shattered my concrete prison with one last push that took everything I had. I could feel Emma's power burning away at every ounce of pressure I summoned, eating away at my mind as it tried to tie me down.

Throwing her away was a gift, but also a necessity.

I slammed my hands together as they came free from the concrete, clapping the dust between them. I pictured a shockwave, focused and lethal, careening above Emma's head. My power complied, shattering the wall behind her and drilling a hole from the basement up to the street.

"Zoe!" Emma shot up from her chair. The clipboard clattered to the ground. I saw her hand drift to her hip, but I caught it in place. "Zoe, we can still fix this. Just—"

"I am fixing this," I growled. She just didn't understand. Could she ever understand?

At least I was giving her the chance to.

"Goodbye, Emma."

"No!"

I threw Emma up and out into the street, and I felt my power surge as she screamed. It was unbelievable; I came back stronger every time they knocked me down. Like every time I—

The door flew open, and Reg followed. I didn't need to look to catch him. He tried to raise a hand to me again. Too bad. He'd been nice to me before. I heard his last thoughts.

Shit

Reg's head splattered against the stone walls of the prison, and he crumpled to the floor.

No more prisons.

My power lashed out, slamming into the walls and cracking them.

No more limits.

The walls buckled.

I had a job to do.

18

Toby - The New Queen

It all started with Emma screaming.

Concrete and asphalt dust poured into the street as the DPR basement erupted outward. The force of the explosion sent shockwaves down the street, shattering windows and sending debris flying. I yelled, but was cut off by the sound of her.

Emma careened through the air, crossing the street in an arc. Her body seemed to defy gravity for a moment, suspended in the chaos. When she was halfway, the surrounding cars stopped mid-drive, freezing in place alongside the seagulls and a billowing cloud of dust.

I ran faster than I ever had before. My feet pounded against the sidewalk, each step a desperate push to reach her in time.

I didn't catch Emma as much as she crashed into my chest, knocking the wind out of me. I threw my arms in the way, using myself as a shield to keep her from hitting the sidewalk. I slammed into the ground instead. I felt something crack in my back, and sharp pain cascaded across my chest as I almost bounced on impact, only held down by Emma's ass against my chest.

Emma stopped screaming and groaned instead. I tried to join her, but the pain in my chest turned it into a cough, which just made it hurt more. Emma rolled off me, which also hurt.

"Fuck," I managed. Emma coughed away dust and tried to stagger to her feet. I found the strength to help her, correcting her jacket and pulling her off the ground. It hurt whenever I moved my right shoulder. Not again.

"Toby?" she asked after a second. Emma was still staring at the building in disbelief. "Are you okay?"

"Kinda," I answered. It'd been between that and 'not sure.'

"Fuck. Fuck. Fuck," Emma swore and stumbled forward, her wide eyes locked on the DPR office. "We need to—" She cut herself off and held out a hand to me. I felt her attention coil in on my chest. All at once, my power let go.

Cars whipped by as time caught up, and then one careened off the road, blurring toward us. It smashed into the wall behind, passing harmlessly through us. The crash happened when we weren't there.

By the time I looked away from the car, I saw the crushed front of the DPR office. The looming brickwork had been torn off the face of the building and scattered across the road. Exposed floor after exposed floor spat out dust and sparking smoke from active wires. Papers fluttered down into the street.

"No, no, no," Emma said. She took several steps toward the building, but the ground shook, and she lost her balance. There was a thunderous boom on the other side of the DPR office, and black, acrid smoke poured from it. "No," Emma repeated, her voice cracked and broke.

I saw a silhouette floating in the middle of the climbing dust and smoke. Her jacket and hood whipped in the wind she'd summoned. Despite the chaos, she was stock still in the air.

Zoe.

Emma shouted the name for me. Calling out.

There was nothing. Zoe was there for one second. Gone the next.

A shattering boom crashed over the city block, shattering windows. I snapped my hands forward and covered Emma's ears at the last second. I almost didn't hear the sound. My ears started ringing immediately, and I staggered back, doubling over. My ribs screamed as I bent, and I dropped to a knee, panting. I could hear my breath in my head, but I couldn't hear anything but ringing beyond it, and the sound was loud enough to almost cloud my vision.

Emma spun around to grab me, and my balance gave way, dropping me onto the sidewalk. After a moment, I had the wherewithal to speak. "Are you okay?" I asked Emma, but I didn't hear the words. I just knew I'd said them.

Emma answered. I might have been perceptive, but I didn't know how to read lips.

I shook my head and then pointed at my ears. Doctors had warned me that I'd be vulnerable to loud noises, but I'd never figured it'd come up like this.

Emma bent down to hug me and pull me off the ground. She was hot. Her breath was panicked and rapid. She was trembling.

I held her back at that moment. Zoe was gone. We weren't in danger, and—

Emma pushed against my embrace for a second, and I winced as she pressed into my ribs. They were definitely cracked, if not broken. After a second of struggle, I felt the first of Emma's rapid breaths break down into sobs. Each one sparked pain up my chest, but that didn't matter.

The fire was licking at the corners of some of the DPR offices now, igniting in places where the paper had touched live wires. I watched the smoke start to join the dust spreading down the street, waiting for the vermilion portal of Rehsman to pop into the space beside us alongside half a dozen agents who'd been prepared for this scenario.

The seconds ticked by.

Then, almost half a minute. I saw the lights from oncoming emergency vehicles bouncing off the buildings further down the street. There was nothing from Rehsman. He wasn't coming.

Had he known this was going to happen? Or at least expected it? I clenched my fist on Emma's back as some of her sobs quieted into deep, shaking breaths. I felt the key to Zoe's office indent on my palm. Had he been telling me to go inside? Had he been trying to get me in there to ensure that—

I couldn't know, and it wasn't the time right now. Was it?

The first ambulance screamed onto the scene. I watched the two paramedics climb out of the vehicle and then stare at the DPR building as the fire climbed up the front walls, skipping from exposed office to exposed office.

Blood was rushing to my ears, replacing some of the ringing. One of the paramedics ran over to us, reaching out and tapping Emma on the shoulder. She turned to the woman just as confusion flashed over her face. I didn't see if Emma'd been injured by the fall, but it wasn't like the paramedic could have healed it if she had.

Emma stood up after exchanging a set of words with the paramedic, giving me an extra squeeze as she did. Love hurt.

There was a crowd forming further down the street now. People who'd escaped from the building mixed with gawkers and onlookers. Emma headed toward it.

The paramedic leaned down in front of me and said something. I was able to grasp that they were asking me a question, but not anything beyond that. I tapped my ear to explain. They nodded, then took a deep breath before resting a hand against my chest. A soothing cool spread out from their palm, covering my chest and then climbing up my skin. Weeks of healing happened all at once, and my hearing stuttered back to life.

The cacophony of sirens and shouts replaced the ringing and smothered the paramedic's next words, but I still understood the intention. He was saying I was lucky that, with how much had just happened, everything was correctable out in the field. After all, it meant my body would have healed itself naturally over time.

I staggered to my feet. I was physically fine, but my body didn't understand that yet and moved in strange ways to try to avoid phantom pains. After a moment, it figured out what was going on, and I stood tall on the side of the street.

More emergency vehicles had arrived. A man poured water onto the building, vomiting it from his mouth. Gross, but useful.

I headed toward the crowd Emma'd gone into, but she emerged from it before I reached it. She'd found Todd.

"Better?" she asked. She was still wincing. I didn't know what she'd hurt, but—"I'm fine, Toby. Really," she said. She must have read my expression. "We just need to..." Her tone told me that when she'd said she was fine, she only meant physically.

"Yeah," I answered her original question and followed up on her response.

"I can't stay here," Emma said. "People need to work."

Emma went to walk away. I was busy staring at Todd. "You okay?" he asked.

I nodded.

"You going to explain what's going on?" was his next question. I stared back at the DPR building and then looked at Emma.

She didn't quite shake her head, offering her opinion, but leaving it up to me.

"Not here," I said once I'd taken my second to think about it. It was too crowded, and we could barely hear each other over the sirens either way.

"I'll grab your bike, Emma," Todd said before heading down the street to where I'd left everything. It wasn't as if we could have fit all three of us on there, let alone driven it out with all the emergency vehicles.

Todd came back carrying the bike under one massive arm. He took it slow, like he was constantly preparing to have it be too heavy for him. As he approached, I felt Emma grab my hand. She dug her nails into the key Rehsman had left me. I felt Emma's attention wash over me in the same way it did when she'd tried to turn off my power, but this time, it was constant, consistent, careful.

Todd reached us and stared at Emma and then at the bike in his arms. Confusion flashed across his face.

Emma nodded.

We really needed to talk.

19

Toby - New Reality

Todd's apartment was closer to the DPR than mine and less likely to draw attention. Of course, it came with the baggage of a very confused Soo-jung, but all things considered, we needed friends in the city. Or at least people we could talk to about it.

Silence hung, letting the bubble of Soo-jung's fish tank filter take over the conversation for a moment. Todd had his arms crossed, staring through the stained glass of a small decoration he'd kept on the window of wherever he'd lived since college. The rain-filtered sunlight streaming through cast colorful patterns on the floor, a sharp contrast to the feeling in the rest of the room.

Todd was frowning, either judging something outside or us. Todd wasn't usually hard to read, but I usually wasn't this nervous when speaking to him.

"I fucking knew it," he said after it had been much too long for polite conversation.

"What?" I asked.

"I fucking knew I had an eye for these things." Todd nodded to himself. I looked at Emma. She was shaking her head, not saying no but accepting the disbelief.

"And everything else?" I prompted. It wasn't quite everything. We'd left out some of the critical details, like wondering what my power could do, if it left a residue on time, that sort of thing. Whatever tests we'd had were destroyed when Zoe'd removed the top floors of the DPR, anyway. So, we would be starting from scratch again.

"Not great from what I understand," Todd said, "but compared to meeting each other? Come on!"

Ignoring everything but the good news. That was incredibly Todd.

"Honey," he continued, "do we have champagne?"

"No," Soo answered. She'd been lingering on the side of the conversation, keeping herself busy while still obviously eavesdropping. For the past few minutes, she'd been organizing the already tidy half bookshelf by the door, her fingers tracing along the spines of color-coded books. "I think you have some gin in the cupboard."

"No thanks," Emma said before I could.

"Yeah, I don't think we're drinking today," I said, "or anytime soon."

"You should be celebrating, guys. Come on. Think about it, you..." Todd sighed. "Actually, this makes complete sense, knowing the two of you. It's the reason I thought it'd go well in the first place."

"I don't think having priorities is a character flaw," Emma said. I nodded along. Todd didn't.

"Having yourself too low on the list of priorities is the flaw," Todd said as he walked away from the window and over to the kitchen. "Having priorities isn't bad. You just need to remember that you're one of them."

Todd and Soo's kitchen wasn't messy, it was just crowded. A thousand little implements and gadgets spread across pegboards and counter-space. It was almost comical watching Todd's massive frame navigate it.

When it was clear that neither Emma nor I were cutting in, Todd continued. "Now that you two have a soulmate, you need to keep them at the top of the priorities list, too. So there are two reasons to drink right now and... What? One to not?"

"Several reasons, at least," I corrected.

"I think Toby and I are considering each other here," Emma said. "We're just happy that we can spend time together at all. That only started today."

"And that is too low a bar," Todd said.

Emma managed half a laugh beside me. Todd was nothing if not disarming.

Todd found the bottle and pulled it down alongside a cavalcade of colorful glasses to choose from. "One drink to celebrate the good times, and then you two can talk about all the other shit to your heart's content." He put his bounty down on one of the few open spaces on the countertop. "Sound good?"

Emma looked at me for guidance. I shrugged. She nodded.

"Perfect," Todd said. He set to pouring, and Soo stopped pretending she wasn't part of this conversation so she could distribute the drinks. Before I knew it, I was staring down at the pine-scented gin. It had adopted the color of the matching sea glass shot cups Soo'd given Emma and me.

Emma caught my frown. "Not a gin person?" she asked quietly enough that Todd couldn't hear as he kept his promise and put the bottle away.

"No. You?"

"Did you see me go for the gin at the bar?" Emma asked. There was the admission. She was a cooler girl.

Todd counted down, and I took a deep breath to steady myself. We started together. Emma sputtered and stopped halfway. I went to grab the drink from her to help, but she kicked it back instead. Offering something close to a smile for my offer.

At least we were getting half smiles. That was all we could really ask for, considering the current circumstances.

"Alright. Business," Todd said with a clap. He grabbed the empty blue and green shot glasses from Emma and me before he pushed us over to the couch-separated area they called a 'living room.' The fish tank took up most of the 'living' space.

Emma and I sat quietly for a moment, almost waiting for Todd to come over. Once he was done with the drink cleanup, he asked

Soo if she needed anything done in the other bedroom or office.

Todd could help how he could, but our explanation had told him that this was above his pay grade, and considering I was jobless, it was certainly above mine. I just didn't have the option of tapping out.

Emma watched Todd leave the room and then sighed. It was split somewhere between contented and a desperate attempt to decompress. Once she'd taken her second, she spoke up. "What were you holding back?" she asked.

"What?"

"When we were talking about Zoe," Emma said, "I said that it was the main issue right now because the samples would have been destroyed in the office, but—"

I held my tongue for a moment. "I don't think I like how well you know me already."

"Soulmates," she said.

I sighed and dug in my pocket, producing the key Rehsman had given me. Emma stared at the key, but didn't seem to recognize it. "Rehsman handed this to me during our conversation after you went in to talk to Zoe." Emma twinged at the mention of that conversation. "Between that and what he said to, I think he knows."

"As in knows what you do? He said that?"

"No," I corrected. "But he certainly knows that something is wrong. He might know everything, or maybe he's just guessing, but he knew about the tests, Emma. I don't think that's a coincidence." The words hung out in the air with the bubbling of the fish tank for a moment, and then I lowered my hand, shoving the key back into my pocket. "So I think we're fucked."

Emma stared at the plush gray rug for a moment. "Not quite."

"Pardon?"

"The Central database for the DPR is in San Francisco," Emma said. "If we can get there, I have the credentials to delete incomplete tests as mis-administered data. Strike it from the record."

"So you could keep the results from getting on the database?" I asked.

Emma nodded.

"But then there is Zoe," I pointed out.

This time, Emma shook her head.

"What?" I asked.

"Toby, we don't have any idea where she is or what she's doing, and you and I can't just walk out into the street and go looking for her," Emma said. "We just saw how that went." The last part was quiet, broken.

"Emma."

"We don't have dispatch on this. Rehsman hasn't said anything about what we're doing about Zoe, and we have no leads, Toby," she said. "Right now, if we think one of your tests is on the central database, we need to get on top of that. It's a problem we can solve."

"The problems keep stacking up, don't they?"

"It all comes from the same one, Toby." Emma sat for a moment. Quiet. Then she spoke up again. "I just don't know how it all started so fast."

"I told you when we were talking to Todd, I gave my name to that canvasser girl."

"Lexi," Emma said.

"What?"

"Lexi. Zoe told me her name. I just didn't think it was worth interrupting during the explanation with Todd." Emma rested her hands on her lap. "That gave them your name, sure, but there were only three people who knew what was going on at that point, Toby. You. Me. Zoe. So how did they get that information?"

"A telepath?" I suggested.

"Zoe was right when she said they wouldn't have been looking. Zoe,"—Emma choked up for a moment.—"Zoe is one of the few telepaths that's ever been strong enough to hear idle thoughts without trying," Emma said, "the other ones we have on record aren't in Crescent. Hell, they're on the other side of the ocean."

"Okay. So where does—"

"There's something we're missing," Emma said, "and—"

"Pardon," Soo said, as she poked her head back into the room. Emma and I both snapped our attention to her instead of spilling more sensitive information.

Of course, the first thing Soo said revealed she'd been listening to everything. It'd been part of the risk of coming to their house. "Toby," she opened, "you said that you were approached by a girl asking you to sign a..." Soo lost the word.

"Petition," Todd called from the other room.

"Petition," she repeated. "They asked you to sign one right after you met Emma for the first time, right?"

"Two days after," I confirmed.

"That happened with me when I met Todd," she said. "Someone came up to me a couple of days later and tried to talk to me about the Department, but my English wasn't very good yet."

"What?" Emma asked.

"Before I'd even gone back to Korea," Soo affirmed.

"You never told me this," Todd joined us in the room.

"I didn't know it wasn't normal," she said. "It happened four more times before I went back home. They kept trying to stop me when I was with my sister. I just thought that was how Crescent was. I'd never been here before."

I stared at Emma. She stared at me.

"Sorry," Soo said.

Emma shook her head. Nobody needed to say sorry, but I imagined that Emma and I were thinking the same thing. If the Red could track people who'd met their soulmates, we needed to get out of Crescent and to San Francisco before they came for us again, and this all spiraled even further out of control.

20

Toby - Quiet Moments

Emma's new ability to stop turning off people's powers nearby if she was focused on me had offered her a new opportunity. For the first time, she was behind the wheel of a car that'd been built sometime in living memory. Despite the novelty, she was frowning at the wheel and had been for the past ten minutes of driving when I'd tried to figure out the music on Todd's old phone, which would have been easier if the damned thing wasn't glacial.

Better than nothing, I supposed.

Emma kept half-staring at the road and half at the wheel as we headed out onto the highway. I knew where the frustration was coming from. I'd argued for a car instead of the bike because I hadn't wanted to hang on for dear life for the entire six hours to San Francisco. Emma must have been picturing something faster than a mid-tier luxury sedan when she'd agreed to the deal.

I spoke up again.

"I can drive."

"You don't drive," she said.

"I drove," I pointed out. "I had a car for years, but I just got rid of it when I moved to Centretown. The place didn't have parking."

"I can drive," she said. "And before you mention it, yes, I'm fine."

"You don't seem fine."

"Just wish I could do more in this thing," Emma said as she

tapped the wheel.

"Like stunt driving?"

"Mhm."

"You've done that?" I asked. Emma nodded and checked the mirrors again. We'd had to adjust them from Todd's height when she'd gotten into the driver's seat. "That's sweet," I said. "Why?"

"Pardon?"

"Why'd you do it?" I asked, sitting up and putting Todd's phone between my legs once I finally figured out how the music worked. There was a neat pocket for a phone in the center console, but Emma's was already there. "Did you think you'd enjoy it?"

"Partially that and partially work," Emma explained. "Is this drive going to be six hours of questions?"

"I was thinking three," I said, "then you can ask me when it's my turn to drive."

Emma frowned at the wheel again, and I watched her try to summon the excitement to participate in real time. She failed. "Just ask. I'll get over this thing"—Emma slapped the steering wheel with her palm again—"in a few minutes."

"So I should ask softballs first so I can hit you with the spicy stuff once you're in a good mood?" I asked. It at least got a chuckle out of her, which pulled a smile from me.

I took a deep breath as we passed the green sign telling us we were leaving Crescent. We didn't know what the city would be like when we returned or exactly when we would be. Hell, we didn't know if we'd be able to come back at all. This would have been a day trip in a perfect world, but...

Well, aside from meeting Emma, how much of this had been a perfect world so far? My best guess was none.

"The questions?" Emma asked once I'd been distracted for a little too long. I nodded and grabbed my phone again, throwing on something Todd had pre-loaded instead of risking a cellular connection.

"Question one," I started.

"We're numbering them?"

"It's an option."

"Was the driving question our question number one, then?" Emma asked as she changed lanes. Pretty soon, we'd start the part of the drive that went along the coast, which would be nice. "Or are we counting the six times you asked me if I was fine or if you should drive?"

"Rude," I said, "and it was nine times."

"I lowballed it for your dignity," Emma said.

"Well, I can't do that, so." I sat up higher in the seat. "How about we start from question one?"

"Sure."

"Okay, question two." It took Emma a second, but she rolled her eyes as she realized I'd counted that as answering a question. Now she was expecting a question, and I'd been focused on the joke. Why, when I needed a question, did every question vanish from my head? I had a near-perfect memory, goddammit. "Favorite animal?"

"Favorite animal?" she repeated. Calling her tone skeptical would have been underselling it. She was incredulous.

"I said I was starting with softballs."

"That's not a softball. That's boring," Emma said. Before I had a chance to disagree with her, she continued. "You don't learn anything about me from that. You just find out what my favorite animal is."

"Well?"

"Snow leopard," she said.

"Why?" I asked. Technically, it was question three, but I was hoping she didn't call me on that.

Emma opened her mouth and then reconsidered the answer twice. Then, after some thought. "You know, I think it's just because I've been saying it since I was six. My parents got me this stupid little picture book. It had a snow leopard on it and now that I'm thinking about it, I think that picture book just made snow leopard the answer, and then eventually it was just the answer because I'd said it every other time. Hm." Emma bit her lip. "Favorite animal might have been a decent question."

"If we're keeping score," I said, "I probably should have asked about your parents..." I watched Emma shake her head as I was speaking, so I let her talk.

"I don't know them that well, haven't seen 'em in seventeen years, babe," she said the last word like it was weird on her tongue. We weren't there yet. "Toby," she self-corrected.

"Seventeen years?"

"They..." she clicked her tongue, and based on history, I knew that wasn't leading to good things. "They weren't that keen to keep me around once my power was manifesting, and, considering what my power was, the DPR was more than happy to step in and—" Emma glanced over at me and clocked my expression. "Look. I'm used to it. Most people in the DPR have a history somewhere like that. Zoe..." Emma sighed, then cursed herself out for bringing up the name again. She took a deep breath and continued, "Zoe moved in with me when I was only fifteen, right? And at that point, she'd accidentally... Well..."

"My parents are down in Florida," I said, to offer a different tone. "They retired early. My mom's a shifter, so she did some modeling, and Dad was a good agent for her. They struck it pretty rich."

"Does your mom still work?" Emma asked. It was a less depressing thread to pull on.

"Took the bag and ran," I said.

"Smart."

"Right?"

"You see them a lot?"

"We talk a lot," I corrected. "Not a whole lot of seeing one another these days, honestly. I haven't been down for about two years."

Emma passed another car on the highway. Despite being in Todd's slow sedan, she was still aiming for record time. The poor green hatchback ate our dust and then was quickly overtaken by the black truck we'd adopted as a study buddy on the way out of Crescent.

"Why?" Emma asked.

"Pardon?"

"Why don't you go see them more?"

"Stuff gets in the way," I said, "it can be pricey and—"

"Toby, we're going to go see your parents when this is all done. Okay?"

"You sure you want to meet them? They made me."

"Are you saying that's a good or a bad thing?"

"Most days, I'm not sure."

"Well, I'm your soulmate, so we're going to see your parents after this. They made something pretty great, in my opinion."

"Something worth it?" I asked.

"Yes," she said a little too fast. We'd both been somewhat clear about it in the past with our interactions. This would all be worth it if it didn't continue to spiral wildly out of control.

The conversation was idle for a while after the parent question. The words weren't careful as the miles dripped by as much as they were simply designed to cut just a little less deep as the sunset threatened.

Eventually, we were getting close to the bay and the beach my parents used to bring me to as a kid. From what I'd heard, it'd gone down the drain in the past years, but it was still a kick of nostalgia in the middle of the drive.

Well, not the middle. We were barely an hour in, but at least the time had been passing pleasantly, even if it wasn't quick.

"Okay," Emma said in response to my most recent explanation, "to be clear. Todd hated you in elementary school?"

"Oh, it was mutual," I said. "He bullied me mercilessly. Complete asshole."

"And then?"

"In high school, he was better, just kind of a dick, and then we ended up at the same university down south, and we were the two kids from Crescent in our dorm."

"Okay? Then you were friends?"

"Yeah, he'd mellowed out a lot over that last summer, and admittedly, I did, too. Next thing we knew, best mates."

"I thought you'd been friends forever based on how he talked about it."

"Friends? No. I've known him forever, but I've only been friends with him for ten-odd years." I shivered at the last part. I didn't have the luxury of forgetting how long it'd been since my days in university.

"Are you sure he doesn't think you were friends the entire time?" Emma asked.

"He'd better not," I said. "We've talked about it before, and we're on the same page, I think."

The sky above us was a stunning mix of setting sun and fading blue, with only a few scattered clouds left from the rain earlier. The coastal highway stretched ahead, bordered by rugged cliffs on one side and the shimmering ocean on the other. I wasn't sure if I was imagining the smell of the ocean or if it was coming through the vents.

I stared in the rearview mirror at the black truck behind us. "Emma, can we pull off at the next exit? There's a rest stop," I said.

"You already need to—"

"No," I said, "I didn't know if you'd noticed, but we've had our friends in the black truck on our tail since Crescent. I can't see inside because of the tinted windows, but—Ah. Nevermind. There's not a lot between here and there. It's probably just..."

"No, you're right, Toby," Emma said. She tracked the truck in her rearview. "We can just pull off for a second to drop them. Worse comes to worst. It's a few minutes. Plus, then I can jump out and—"

"You were just giving me shit for wanting to pull over," I pointed out.

"We're already going to be pulling over. It's different from asking," she said. Emma still had her eyes locked on the black truck in her rearview.

We approached the exit. She was whispering to herself.

Emma flicked on her signal and got over to the exit lane. The truck echoed the move. It wasn't a subtle tail, but Emma swore either way.

I swore when the car behind it also signaled and pulled off with us.

Couldn't get one car ride of peace.

21

Zoe - Scattered

I dropped to my knees, my fingers splashing in the blood on the floor and my fingernails digging into the linoleum. Above, a broken light fixture sparked, raining down on me. Each of the sparks danced in the air, avoiding actually making contact with my skin.

I took a deep, gulping breath, gasping for air. I could taste the metallic scent of blood and the acrid sting of burnt wiring. The place was a warzone; I'd woken up on the floor on the other side of the room, collapsed between two bodies that'd been split between the four corners of the house. I wasn't sure where I was, and I wasn't sure how long it'd been since I'd blacked out.

The linoleum stabbed me as I dug my fingernails further into the floor. How long had it been since the DPR? How much had I done since then? How—the sun had set outside. Just barely, from the looks of it, but...

It would have helped if I knew what day it was.

I tried to push myself off the floor with my mind, but it abandoned me again, scattering to the wind until I jumped back on the wagon and engaged in the plan. In my—its—our purpose. We had a goal, and I was being weak right now. It was my fault that my power wasn't here to support me. I had to deliver on my end as well.

But I needed time. I needed a minute. I wasn't holding back anymore. I was using so much more of my power than I was used to. There were so many corners of my mind I hadn't plundered for energy. There were so many places I hadn't considered before. So many ways to...

So many ways to do whatever I wanted.

Whatever we wanted.

I shook my head. Why had I never heard the second voice before? The poking and prodding of my power had always been suggestions. Whispers in the back of my head and prickling under my skin as opposed to the bold, confident instinct I understood now.

This was how I always should have been. I should have been letting loose from day one. How many problems could I have solved over the years if I hadn't been so scared? If I hadn't been a coward? If I'd faced the truth instead of hiding away from it...

I wouldn't have died. I couldn't have died.

My body found the strength, and I staggered to my feet, using the cracked drywall of the suburban house as support. The blood stained the paint there, too. Was that from my hand or from before?

Didn't matter.

My power lashed out in a random direction, cracking against a side table, one of the few pieces of furniture I hadn't already broken in the room. The wood splintered at the first mental lash and then disassembled itself while floating in midair, each piece snapping over and over until it was a pile of splinters and sawdust. I held out my hand, calling some of the scattered shards over.

My power refused. It wanted to do one thing and one thing only right now. It needed to hunt. It wanted to.

And I knew. I knew what it wanted to do. I wanted to do it too. We were so close to fixing things. We were so close to crossing everyone off our list, and once I'd done that, I could go back. Everything would be fixed. Emma would apologize. Toby would be safe. The Red would be dead.

Well, it wouldn't all be the same. I wouldn't hold back anymore, and everyone would know. Everyone would stay the fuck out of my city once they understood what I could do. Someone as useless as Kris wouldn't be able to summon people to his cause because everyone would know the price they'd pay for defying me.

Right now, though? Right now, I needed to rest. No. I didn't need to rest. My weak body needed to rest. It needed food. Needed breaks. It was holding me back, I just—

My hand drifted to my cheek. I didn't know when the bandage had come off, but my nails ran down the familiar cuts I'd carved. I dug my nails in again, pushing past the scabs that'd formed when I was sleeping. Blood welled on my skin, first droplets, then a stream.

That was better. I knew what my cheek was supposed to look like, and it wasn't perfect and smooth.

Pain shot across my face as I pulled my hand away. Just another way my body was weak.

I tried to walk across the house to the kitchen and my steps faltered in the dark, shattered hallway. The house looked like it'd been a typical suburban sanctuary with cozy, plush furniture and family photographs, but the fight had ruined everything. Down the hallway, blood was smeared across the once-pristine walls in haphazard patterns, and on the floor, a shattered silver mirror was face down.

I just needed to get across the house and I could... I felt my steps wobble and falter before I'd even threatened to take another stable one. I leaned against the blood-slicked wall. I didn't have the energy for this. I just needed—

Yes.

I took a deep breath and closed my eyes, casting a mental net over the block, then the suburb, then the city, then beyond. My power offered to reach as far as I needed as long as I was hunting. And I was hunting. I just wasn't hunting for the Red right now. I was hunting for a solution.

I was out the window before I even registered where I was going, shattering the glass outward into the fading evening. Then I was off like a shot. Up. North. Through the sound barrier and the clear sky.

By the time I understood where I was headed, my power had already brought me there. I touched down on the ground outside a ramshackle house on the edge of Crescent. The warm glow from inside spilled out onto the sidewalk. The neighborhood was too old to have streetlamps, so it was the only thing illuminating me.

I knocked on the door from several feet away, but didn't wait for the answer. My mind punched through the lock, twisting and breaking the door frame. Wood shot into the front hallway and landed in the disorganized pile of sneakers on the floor. The pile of shoes started tearing itself apart just as I saw a face at the end of the hallway.

The boy's eyes widened, but he turned too late. I held out a hand and summoned him. He flew down the hall, snapping to a spine-shattering stop a foot short of me. His worn-out shirt frayed at the edges as I held him in the air.

He opened his mouth to scream. I held it shut.

"Shh," I said. My voice had been hoarse since the DPR. It sounded right. It sounded how it had when I'd been screaming on the ground. When I—When I'd—The boy winced as I pressed too hard on his jaw. I felt teeth crack.

No. I needed him.

"Shh," I repeated. His eyes were still wild and panicked. "You're safe. You're with me," I said.

His thoughts told me he didn't find that as reassuring as he should have.

"I'm not crazy, you're just—" I hissed. My power started applying pressure to his chest, threatening his ribs second by second and—

No. I needed him.

I forced myself to let go, and the boy dropped to the ground, coughing and sputtering at my feet. I crouched to meet him. "I'm from the Department of Power Control," I said. "I'm hurt. I need you to fix me. To help me. Can you do that?"

He didn't nod, so I made him.

"Good. Glad we're on the same page," I said.

The boy's eyes darted to the cut on my cheek. The drywall on either side of the hallway caved in.

"Not. That."

The boy's eyes stayed wide, but he nodded rapidly. This time, he didn't need my help.

"Good," I said.

The boy put a shaking hand on my sternum, first his fingers, then his palm. I held his wrist in place. The shaking slithered up to his shoulders instead of his hand.

"You don't need to be scared." I explained. "You haven't done anything wrong. It's all of them that need to be scared." I nodded, along with his thoughts. "You don't know who they are," I said. "That's fine. You don't need to. They won't be around much longer."

He had his hand on my chest, but I didn't feel the cooling presence of a healer under my skin. I pushed deeper into his thoughts. The doorknob on the broken door crumpled in on itself as I read.

"I am going to hurt people," I affirmed, "but they're the right people. The people who don't want everyone to be safe," I said. The light fixture swung back and forth on the ceiling before the chain pulled too far, revealing raw wiring. "Didn't you hear me before? I'm with the DPR. We're the good guys. At least most of us. Some of them got in my way and..."

The kid was still hesitating. For a second, it almost felt like he was trying to pull his hand away.

"Are you getting in my way?" I snapped, "or are you going to help me keep people safe?"

The boy swallowed. My power stepped in the way of his Adam's apple and held it in place. After a second, the cool relief of a healer started building in my chest, pulling away the aches and pains.

There was still more work to be done; once I was better, I'd open up my mind. I'd felt it, the offer to go even further afield. The power to search beyond Crescent's borders.

There was nowhere to hide, and I had names on my list.

22

Toby - Resisting Arrest

Emma took a deep breath as she slammed her back against the underside of the counter, getting low with me as the three Redcoats entered the restaurant through the hole we'd broken in the window. We'd run in here as soon as we'd seen them get out of the cars behind us. The uniforms had made them easy to spot. I guess we were past the point of subtlety.

There had been a twinge of guilt in the back of my head when Emma'd broken the window of the small, family-run restaurant at the rest stop open, but the door had been locked, and she needed the Red to get close. We couldn't fight outside.

Still, the sign outside the restaurant had been so charming. Hopefully, we wouldn't ruin too much of the interior.

Emma steadied herself, and her hand shot to her hip. She pulled out a pistol, taking a moment to eject the magazine and ensure that there were bullets inside. Once she was satisfied, she spun the gun in her hand and offered the handle to me.

I didn't take it.

Emma shook it in my direction to repeat the offer without speaking. There weren't many hiding places here, so they would find us, but speaking would have cost us precious seconds.

I shook my head. I couldn't. I wasn't going to do that. I didn't want to kill.

Again.

Emma scanned my face for a moment, reading my reaction, and then spun the gun back around. She silently swore, only mouthing the words but fully summoning the intent.

I heard a third set of boots on glass.

Emma caught my contemplation and raised her eyebrows. I held up my fingers to relay the information, and she nodded to herself. Her expression was calm and analytical, quiet and calculated. How was she so ready for this?

I knew the answer. It was because she'd done this before.

One of the Red behind us stepped a little too loudly, marking their location. I wanted to turn to look. Emma sprang into action.

When I'd seen Emma vault over the counter at the bar, I'd called it graceful. Now I knew where that came from. She swung over the countertop with deadly ease, rushing into the table-filled dining area. I followed, but ran around the counter instead.

The closest Red, the man we'd seen outside with the scarred cheek, lashed out when Emma was way too far away. Confusion flashed across his face before it was too late. Emma was on top of him, and she leapt off the ground, cracking her elbow into his face and shattering his nose. I heard the spurting gurgle of blood and cartilage pouring onto the floor.

The man yelped. Emma drew the attention of the two others in the room and snapped to meet it. I crossed the distance to the man she'd just hit as he stumbled backward.

Emma'd said it when I'd asked her about the motorcycle. She considered her power an equalizer, but she was the only person training for situations without their power. She stripped everything away and then ensured nobody in the room was ready for her.

I slammed into the man as he started to regain his balance, throwing him into the old wooden table in the middle of the room. I heard the legs crack under our combined weight as I followed him onto the tabletop.

A gunshot.

Emma snapped my attention away as one man screamed, dropping to the ground as his right kneecap vaporized. He'd been twice Emma's height before, but once he dropped to the sticky tile floor, he was just close enough to—

My new friend grabbed at my collar, trying to wrestle me off the table. I found a second to free my hand and knew the best target. Blood splattered over my knuckles as I slammed him in the already broken nose. There was so much already. There was so much—

I hesitated for too long, and the man threw me down to the tile. I saw Emma's motorcycle boots from my space under the table as she kicked at someone in the room. I couldn't tell who. I'd slammed my head too hard on the ground. Everything was blurry.

The scarred man staggered off the table, holding his nose. He shouted, his voice broken as his face was. "Deb, what the fuck are you doing?"

The woman in the room, who, based on the fact that I hadn't heard her scream, was the only one who'd offered any resistance to Emma's assault, yelled back. "It's not fucking working."

"What do you mean it's not—" Emma cut the man off with a knee to the back as he stared at me. He fell forward, but Emma snatched his wrists, holding him in place for a moment. Blood from his nose dripped down and landed beside my ear.

"Alright," Emma started. She spun the man around as she spoke, using his arm as leverage. In half a second, she had him pinned to the table I'd had him on earlier with her gun to his temple. She'd only fired one shot, which meant it was still loaded. "Shut the fuck up. All of you."

On one hand, what a woman. On the other hand, terrifying. That had been too many of my experiences with Emma so far. Maybe I had a complex I didn't know about.

"Just calm down," the woman said on the other side of the room. She had an empty knife holster on her shoulder and a knife sticking out of her arm. Brutal.

"Calm down?" Emma asked. "We didn't start this." As she said 'we,' she nodded to me. I got up to join her. "I'm offering to talk." She pushed the gun into the man's temple, leaving a red mark on the surrounding skin as he bled onto the table. "This is me being calm," she finished.

The woman raised the arm that didn't have a knife in it, and the large man kept both hands on his missing kneecap. He whimpered. I looked at Emma; she was scanning them both.

"Okay," she said after a second, "does someone here want to explain why the fuck you were following us?"

Emma waited. The woman looked down at the bigger man, who was too trapped in pain to speak, and then she looked at the man on the table but didn't talk.

"What about you?" Emma asked, leaning down to the man she was threatening. "Is this really worth it? You're that loyal to the cause that you'd—"

I cut Emma off by putting a hand on her shoulder. She caught me shaking my head. She wouldn't execute someone, would she?

"Don't make me kill you in front of him." Emma's tone had changed almost imperceptibly. "My boyfriend really wouldn't like that." She'd been bluffing, and now she was making it obvious to me, but I doubted anyone else could tell.

"We're just trying to talk."

"Nice talk then," Emma hissed. "You used that line last time, didn't you? Back in Crescent. What happened then?"

The table groaned as the man struggled under Emma, but one twist of the pistol stopped his wriggling.

"Look," the woman said, "this has all gotten out of control. We weren't trying to do any of this. We were just following you and—"

"Does someone here want to give me a straight answer? Because I'm really running out of patience." Emma looked at me. I could see a plan behind her eyes. "Wanna know what? Take a walk, Toby. I'll be done with them in a minute."

"Emma?"

"Not sure you want to be in the room for this," Emma said. I didn't know exactly what gave it away, but I understood she wanted me to play along.

"Okay." I put my hands up and backed away. I didn't know how

Emma would do it, but based on the competence I'd just seen, I was sure she'd get what we needed. I walked toward the back of the building, considering the front was where everyone had come from.

I took a deep breath and the dim light of the storeroom flickered above me as I passed shelves stacked with canned goods and cleaning supplies. The smell of stale bread and industrial cleaner filled the air, mixing with the lingering stink of frying oil from the kitchen. I pushed open and walked out the back door, putting two pieces of metal between Emma and myself. The chilly evening air was a slap in the face compared to the stuffy interior of the closed restaurant. It almost woke me up from the adrenaline spike I'd been riding.

I didn't know what I'd expected from seeing her in action, but that hadn't been it. I'd been fumbling in there when Emma had been lethally efficient, and... well, it was clear that if I hadn't been in the room, Emma could have been literally lethal to them if she wanted to be, shooting something other than kneecaps.

I kept my ears open for a second, trying to hear what was happening in the other room, but I was too far. I took a deep breath of the air instead. It was nice to be out of the city. I didn't do it enough, even if circumstances were...suboptimal.

Maybe I'd been naïve to think that Emma would have been anything other than deadly. She was part of the DPR, and they were always clear about what happened within their walls. They tried to keep everyone around. They tried to arrest and capture, but—

Well, Zoe'd been scary at the start of the week for a reason. Now, I didn't even know what to call her. Scary didn't seem to cut it. At least we'd put some distance between ourselves and her and got outside of her mental net.

Or maybe, more pointedly, we thankfully weren't her target.

I took a few more steps away from the restaurant, putting more distance between myself and the fight. Once we were in San Francisco, we could erase the record that Rehsman had probably made from the central database of the DPR, but what about after that? Emma had said that Zoe wasn't the focus right now, but she had to be the focus next, didn't she?

Maybe the Red and Kris Allens were the next step? Maybe Zoe and them would burn each other out. That was probably what Rehsman, and the DPR wanted, though they couldn't admit it on paper, and Emma didn't want to. Zoe was always taking care of problems; now, she was just doing it in a way that let them deny their involvement.

I took one more deep breath, the crisp air filling my lungs and helping to clear my head. It had probably been long enough for me to join Emma and figure out what she knew.

The world stuttered with my first steps toward the back door. I'd walked a little too far. I sighed. We'd have to test for the exact range when we had time. I jogged the rest of the way, getting back through the storeroom and into the main area of the restaurant. Emma was tapping her foot on the ground, waiting for me.

"Get what you needed?" I asked.

"Not really," she sighed, glancing around the now quiet room. "They don't seem to know a lot. Just following a bunch of orders from people who aren't here."

The smell of gunpowder from Emma's one shot lingered in the air, and blood stained the tile. But for the most part, we'd avoided destroying the restaurant in the fight.

"So, what's the plan? We can't just leave like this. Can we?" I asked.

"We could, but then they'd just follow us all the way to the city," Emma said. "Can't let that happen."

"Emma—"

"I'm not suggesting I shoot them, Toby. I'm saying that we need to call them in," she explained. "Maybe one shot in the girl's foot to keep her from running in the meantime."

I cringed at the last part.

"Hey," Emma said, "I know this is new to you, but fights like this aren't pretty. If it weren't for healers, a lot more people would die on both sides. Injure and capture's the best we got." Emma crossed over to me, leaving the still form of the broken-nosed man on the table. "And that's part of the reason we're doing all this, so you don't have to get involved in my work." She rested a hand on my cheek, and I smirked. I was starting to understand her physical habits.

I brushed away the hand to let her know I was okay. "I know, it's just—"

"It's new," Emma said.

"Yeah. That."

"Ready?" she asked as she walked back over to the man. We didn't know 100% what would happen when we stuttered back in time. Would Emma already shot the people in the legs? Did the fact that she hadn't done it in our frozen space mean that they'd suddenly be healed?

I nodded.

Emma closed her eyes, and I felt her focus wash over me.

Dust and glass shattered around us as time caught up. Fire tore through the space, and I dove for Emma. We crashed to the ground as the table under her shattered, having broken in the time we were gone. What the hell had—

I looked up toward the front of the restaurant, where the happy small-town wooden sign was charred and splintered. I recognized the man there. Kris.

Kris whipped around as I tried to pull Emma up, but Emma was the fastest of us. She snapped the pistol into place, and it cracked four times. The last two embedded themselves in the wall, and the first two shattered against a barrier wrapped around him.

I jumped to my feet, and Emma matched. The girl beside Kris, the canvasser from before, Lexi, spun and held her hands out. A shimmering translucent barrier formed and then stuttered between us. I saw her struggling, trying to maintain it so close to Emma.

Kris looked to a spot on the floor where a set of handcuffs was sitting empty, then back to Emma and me. The confused sounds of people realizing they hadn't been shot were barely louder than the crackling fire. There was a moment of quiet. Emma's eyes were darting back and forth as she tried to find a hole in Lexi's shield.

"Now, what the hell just happened?" Kris asked after a second.

He looked from me to Emma, then back to me. "How about you put the gun down?" he continued.

Emma didn't justify that with words.

In the quiet, pain had time to seep in, a searing burn on my palm that—The same thing had happened back when I'd saved Zoe. My arm got dislocated just as time caught up. I must have felt however I'd gotten hurt, no matter which 'time' it happened in.

Kris cocked his head at Emma. "Okay. If you wanna waste the last two shots, you can. But I want to know how you keep doing that." He turned his attention to me.

"Doing what?" I asked.

"This is the second time we've had you pinned down, and you've disappeared, and you don't teleport."

It was my turn to cock my head at him. Did they not know? They'd followed me out at the bar. Them coming after me was the whole reason that—

Emma shot her second hand up, and the shield dropped. She pulled the trigger the last two times. Kris shattered into sparks as the bullets hit. He reformed several inches away. I could see the holes in his jacket where Emma's bullets had punched through, but there was only bruising under it.

He was just a little too fast. The man's brow furrowed, and he patted himself where the bullets had hit, checking that they weren't in him.

Sweat dripped down Emma's forehead, and she dropped the hand. The translucent barrier in the middle of the room sparked back to life.

"So that's how it works," Kris said.

Emma threw away the gun and held up her hands. I matched her after a second.

After all, they'd promised that they just wanted to talk.

23

Toby - Plots

Night fell over the next half hour of the drive, but Lexi and Kris had checked Emma and me into a shoddy motel on the far side of Arcata Bay Bridge. The place had been built in the early days of powers, set up to accommodate the military bases there, back when there'd been a more formal military, with guns and tanks and such.

The room smelled like mildew and disappointment, and its appearance matched. Most people knew hotels put multicolored blankets on top of the bed to hide the stains that would have formed otherwise, but this one had managed to get dirt through the pattern. The wallpaper peeled at the corners on each wall of the room, revealing patches that might have been mold but were hopefully just rancid grime.

At the moment, Emma and I were curled up in the bathroom on either side of the porcelain tub because, at least with enough scrubbing from the mini-soaps, it'd felt like a place we could sit down. I was sitting up on the tub's edge, with the still-water-stained faucet digging into my back. Emma had slumped down into the tub itself, her legs folded uncomfortably to allow me any space for my feet.

We understood we were ostensibly prisoners, but this felt cruel and unusual, especially as the minutes dragged into hours.

There was a man posted outside. At least, I thought it was a man based on the sound of his footsteps. Outside of that, though? No security.

Well, save for the fact that they'd taken all our stuff, and we knew Lexi and Kris were in the same building.

If the room had been a little larger, or I'd been a little more stressed, we could have begun the time stop and slipped back into the world. Now, instead, here we were.

"Still not feeling it yet?" Emma asked.

I shook my head.

"Fuck."

"How long do we have to get to San Francisco?" I asked.

"Depends on when he submitted the test, but—I wouldn't want to leave it longer than tomorrow. To be safe."

"And if the test gets on there, it's—"

"Whatever information is on it gets added to the database, good or bad."

"So we're just rolling the dice if that happens?" I asked.

Emma didn't respond with words. Instead, I got a simple "Mhm."

I fidgeted with the knobs behind me, turning them back and forth in the minuscule wiggle zone before they called water. "And if we can't do my thing?" I asked.

"If I can do what I did to Lexi again and focus on one person," she started, "maybe we can take Kris. But all of them? It seems like Kris was free to do whatever he wanted when I had my focus on Lexi, so—"

"You think it's selective or general, right? You don't get both."

"Make it hard on everyone or turn someone really strong completely off," Emma confirmed. "Seems like those are my options."

I sighed. "So either I figure out how to stop time here, or we try to fight them and lose?" I asked.

"Or we sleep here in the tub," Emma offered as a third option.

I stared at the pile of soaked towels we'd stacked in the corner after using them to clean the tub. "That's the worst one," I said.

Emma nodded.

Someone knocked on the door.

Emma sat up and the door creaked open without getting answered, and the man stationed outside held it ajar for Kris and Lexi. Kris's fancy shoes stood out against the worn carpet as they walked in. The pair checked the bed before realizing that Emma and I were tucked in the washroom.

Kris laughed. Lexi didn't.

"Hope it hasn't been too long," Kris said as he approached. I could almost feel Emma simmering beside me. If there'd been water in the tub, she would have evaporated it. "We're just trying to figure out logistics."

"Logistics of what?" Emma asked. "Bet you guys are getting torn apart out there."

Kris frowned at the accusation. "Is that your stance?"

"Were you looking for a cheerleader?" she asked. I shot Emma a look, but she either missed or ignored it. I didn't want to piss Kris off to where he decided we weren't worth it.

"We went through too much trouble to arrange this conversation, Ms. Tavish. Let's not make more," Kris said. As he finished, he reached into the pocket of his signature red coat and pulled out a pack of cigarettes. He turned the open side to us.

I shook my head. Emma considered it for a little longer, but eventually matched me.

Kris shrugged and pulled out a cigarette; he lit it by coughing.

Had that all been a show to flex that he could still use his power with Emma around?

"You said you wanted to talk to me," I said. "Now we're here."

"I'd wanted you alone, Mr. Vander," Kris said, "but you have a nasty habit of vanishing as soon as we get a grip on you. Making it almost like you'd never been there at all."

"You'd never seen that trick when you first tried talking to him," Emma said.

"No, we hadn't, between that and your friend, Zoe—"

"The bitch," Lexi cut in. She caught a glare from everyone else in the room for it.

"Zoe," Kris repeated, "this has been more of a pain in our ass than we ever wanted."

"Why talk to Toby?" Emma asked. "What's so interesting about him?"

"Well,"—Kris snapped a finger, and a pack of matches burned on the other side of the room—"Now there's a lot I want to ask you, Toby, but before? Before, we'd just wanted to speak to Toby as an avenue to get you to Emma."

Emma couldn't help herself. A single broken laugh escaped her lips.

So what? This had all been an accident? They were never coming for me? They'd just wanted to use me to get to Emma once they discovered we were soulmates.

"Oh my God," Emma managed, barely wheezing the words.

Kris and Lexi didn't understand what was so funny. I understood the context, but I still wasn't sure it was funny myself.

"I feel like I'm being left out of a joke," Kris said after a moment. The pair of them were looming over us as Emma laughed. It was the first time I'd really gotten a chance to analyze either moving face. Lexi was so much younger than Kris. It had to be at the edge of the soulmate bounds. "Care to explain, Emma?" he asked.

Emma took a moment to cool. I could almost see the words on her lips. She wanted to mock them for not knowing what I did. We'd been so scared of what they wanted with me that we hadn't thought of any other scenario. Why would we? They'd attacked me in the street. "Why would you want me?" she asked.

"Why would we want McCourtney's leash?" Kris asked rhetorically, "Having just met her soulmate? You could have been the only solution to our Zoe problem. At least the only assured one."

"Zoe problem?" I asked.

"We were close to ready, but that bitch—"

Kris cut Lexi off. "We never found a solution to Zoe's

involvement within the Department of Power Regulation," Kris said. "We've found that reaching out to members of the DPR in other cities via their soulmates was an effective way of recruiting. After all, they're all already mostly high-level and are stressed about the implications of a soulmate. Does that sound familiar?"

"You had people on the inside," Emma said. I could hear the hurt in her voice, the way it shook.

"Have," Kris corrected. "Mind you, not in Crescent, because McCourtney could have sniffed them out." The man sighed and walked back to the central part of the hotel room, stopping at the desk that had only been half-ass-wet-wiped for the past ten years. He grabbed a chair and brought it over so he could meet us at our level. "We have a wide network, Emma, wider than you knew. If Zoe is hunting down everyone affiliated or associated..." he'd trailed off intentionally to let the point sink in. "If she began hunting down everyone sympathetic? Where would she stop?"

"So what?" Emma asked. "She's the one thing in the way of your little revolution, and you want us to help you take care of her?"

"That was going to be our pitch through Mr. Vander here, but no." Kris leaned in. "We want you to help us stop Zoe because she's out of control."

"And then you have your little revolution, right?" I asked. Kris frowned at that, but Emma smiled at me. "Sounds like we're trading one devil for another."

"You've seen what that maniac is doing. Don't compare us," Lexi said. There was genuine hate behind her voice this time. "I watched her kill my friends, and before that, she locked—"

"Unfortunately, this can't be just a personal vendetta," Kris cut Lexi off again, but I'd seen where she was going. Kris only wanted us to hear about the poor victim instead of the girl who'd wanted Zoe gone from the start. "This is combining our powers to protect people."

"Why don't you just try again without us?" Emma asked. "You got her pretty good the first time." Her tone was baiting. Taunting.

It didn't work on Lexi because she couldn't get any angrier, and

Kris took a deep breath, letting it wash off him. "That was a miracle, with the element of surprise, and, as we can all tell, it didn't stick." Kris took a drag from the cigarette and held it for a long time before exhaling the smoke. "We had Toby. We thought Zoe was dead, and then suddenly, neither of those were true."

Emma bit her lip and didn't offer words. I joined her in silence.

"So, considering I could only surprise Zoe with my dearest wife here once," Kris explained, "we're back in a bind. If you join us, we can assuredly stop her rampage and—"

"No, you're just gonna step in—" Emma started, but looked aghast when Kris held a finger up to quiet her. Now she knew what it felt like.

"I'm finishing my pitch here," Kris said. "We want your help keeping Zoe on the ground when she comes for us. We'll arrange a coordinated assault, and you simply need to weaken her as much as possible—"

"Why should we make a deal if it just puts you in charge?" I asked.

I felt the room get hotter as Kris took another deep breath to stabilize himself. Emma pressed her heel against mine in the tub to let me know she appreciated my contribution.

"If you'd allow me to finish," Kris said. "Here's my full pitch. We have people inside the Department of Power Regulation, many in the San Francisco office. You help us, and we'll have our people on the inside wipe records of anything going on with Toby and you over the past week from the database. Hell, we can expunge you from the Dangerous Powers Database completely. Wouldn't be the first time." Kris turned his attention to Emma. "Though your relationship with Mr. Rehsman may make that difficult in your case, Emma."

Emma stared at the tub floor, and I felt her heel press harder into mine. It was the perfect offer, wasn't it? We got everything we wanted, and we could help get Zoe under control and—

Emma looked at me. She didn't need to shake her head for me to understand we weren't there yet.

"We capture Zoe alive," I added as a caveat.

It was Emma who spoke up first. "That might not be possible," she said. "I can't keep her down. Who could?"

"See, she gets it," Lexi said.

Emma glared.

"So?" Kris prompted.

Emma, throughout the conversation, had been sliding lower and lower in the tub to manage foot-to-foot contact with me. She sat up. "One caveat."

Kris perked up. "Yes?"

"You turn yourselves in after," Emma said.

"The entire organization?" Kris scoffed.

"You two," Emma corrected. "If we help your plan. We do our best to keep Zoe alive. You wipe us from the database. Then, you two turn yourselves into the DPR. You don't get to just walk away from this. Not after everything you caused."

Kris frowned. Then he leaned forward, steepling his hands and sighing through them.

"It's that, or try your luck with Zoe," Emma said.

"Fuck off, we're not doing that," Lexi snapped. "She's tried to kill me twice! I'm not getting thrown in jail because she's a psychotic—"

"Might be better than the alternative," Kris said. "Lexi. We should speak about this."

"You're kidding, right?"

"No. I'm not."

Once Lexi realized Kris was taking the offer seriously, she softened. God, she was young. Kris stood up, and the remainder of his cigarette turned to ash between his fingertips. "Can we have some time to consider your offer?" He took time to look at both of us as he asked. I nodded first. "You should consider alternatives in case we're at an impasse."

"Sure," Emma said. I could tell she was lying, and Kris likely could as well. That said, Kris offered another nod before heading out of the room. Lexi followed, looking like she'd hated every minute of this.

The offer was on the table. I stared into Emma's gorgeous eyes as she considered it, and we were alone in the room again.

24

Toby - All Great Plans

"You know," I said as the pain started to really set into the back of my neck, "if you'd told me this was what my first overnight stay with my soulmate would be like…" I considered how to finish the comment. "Well, I don't think I would have been very happy about it."

Over the past few hours, I'd slid down into the tub and joined Emma, forcing her mostly on top of me to ensure that we both fit in the space. At a different time and in any other place, this might have been the start of a romantic evening, but right now, we were both just trying to live through it.

"Do you think they're going to take the offer?" Emma asked.

"Here's hoping," I said. We'd gotten to that point several times, but we'd always stopped there. I kept going. "Do we follow through if they do?"

"Do we have a choice?"

"Escape as soon as we get the chance?" I suggested.

"Toby," Emma said from her spot partially on top of me in the tub, "I don't want to bring down the stellar mood,"—she dripped as much sarcasm on the words as she could—"but that doesn't solve all our problems. Even if we get to San Francisco and do everything there, Zoe is still—"

"We can figure out something for Zoe."

"Toby" was all Emma said, but there was a novel hidden in the tone. That said, of all the chapters, a single one stood out to me: resignation, followed by understanding. We'd tried to keep it light in the car, but that meant I hadn't had a good chance to help Emma through this, and from the sound of it, she needed the help. I took a deep breath.

"Emma."

"No," she said, "I'm not okay, but no. I don't want to talk about it."

I stared at the flickering light fixture on the bathroom ceiling. It washed the entire room in an eerie pale glow, but neither of us wanted to touch the switch to turn it off. The grout between the bathroom tiles was dark with grime, and the switch was somehow worse. "Maybe we should talk about it anyway," I said.

Emma sighed. "Who are you, my therapist?"

"You go to therapy?"

"You don't?"

"What's that supposed to mean?"

"Nothing, I just expected—"

The ground shook, then the walls shook. "What the fuck?" I asked as I tried to sit up. The ground shook again in the time it took Emma and me to untangle ourselves and jump to our feet.

I ran out of the bathroom over to the window, but it was too grime-covered to see through. I swore. Emma pounded on the door.

No answer.

The room rattled again, but this time, it wasn't the ground shaking; it was just the building.

"Fuck it," I tried the door, and though the knob turned, something was blocking it on the other side. "Shit." I kicked the door, to no avail. The tremors rocketed up the walls again.

Emma had grabbed the chair Kris pulled into the washroom earlier. She threw it at the window, breaking the vintage glass in a single massive shatter. Emma smiled at the carnage.

I made a mental note to never suggest a glass table.

The building shook again, and we both made it out the window,

Emma vaulting over and me carefully climbing while double-checking for shards of glass.

The night air was cool compared to the stifling hotel room. A light ocean breeze carried the smell of salt on the wind. If we hadn't been locked inside, this really could have been a romantic evening.

"What's going on?" Emma asked a second before I could. The building had been shaking, but there was a distinct lack of chaos.

I heard it first and grabbed Emma by the back of the neck to shove her down.

We hadn't needed to duck, but a man screamed, flying from the roof of the motel at Mach speed before splattering on the parking lot, repainting half the empty spots with his smeared blood.

"Toby, the cars."

Firelight erupted on the top of the hotel, washing the entire scene in hellish orange. With the added illumination, I saw additional bodies strewn on the gravel road beyond the parking lot. As the fire died, the corpses slipped back into shadow.

"Wait," I said. Emma had just taken the first steps toward the stairway. "When we got here, I saw what room Kris and Lexi went into and—"

"Toby, we don't have time." The building shook to stress Emma's point. Now that I was outside and had my feet on the ground, I could tell that it was all on the other side for the time being.

"Emma, our stuff is in there."

"Toby."

"And probably the keys to any of these cars."

Emma swore and let me lead. I took off down the never-washed outdoor hallway of the motel, reaching the stairway in near-record time. On the first flight, I jumped down the last three stairs and, on the second, leaped down the last four, crashing to the ground just as it shook again. This time, I watched the ancient timber of the building buckle.

Shit.

I ran to the room I'd seen Lexi and Kris head into when we'd gotten to the motel and the door was missing. The doorframe was charred and splintered where Kris had blasted it open.

Emma and I peeled into the room. They'd been kind enough to leave our things on the desk at the front. Emma reached them first, grabbing the gun off the counter and throwing Zoe's switchblade back at me. I flinched as I caught it, almost dropping the thing.

Once we had our stuff in our pockets, I checked one side of the drawers and pulled out the keys. Emma checked hers and grabbed a gun, which was presumably Lexi's, and shoved it into her waistband.

Emma caught me staring and pulled the gun out, turning it around to me again.

I almost shook my head... but it was safer in my pocket than in her waistband. I grabbed the gun from her, and Emma nodded. A second later, she had a small pile of magazines in her arms, holding them out to me as well. "These, too."

"Sure," I grabbed them and shoved them into the pockets they'd squeeze into. When I'd dressed for the day, I hadn't planned on being on the run. I was just lucky Emma had made me take my jacket back during our meeting in the office. Otherwise, I would have been lethally short on carry capacity.

The building shook, and plaster cracked off the ceiling, clattering to the already dusty patterned carpet. If there was one building Zoe was going to destroy tonight, I hoped it would be this fucking motel.

I pressed the lock button on the car key, and headlights lit up in the parking lot, revealing a car with a nasty dent in the side where a woman had been thrown into it.

Beggars and choosers.

I ran back into the night, across the dying 'lawn' of the motel and onto the cracked, rough pavement of the parking lot. We slowed as we heard a yell above us. I was standing in front of the stain we'd seen made when we'd come outside.

Everything that was left of a person.

"Toby, come on." Emma put a hand on my shoulder and pushed as she walked around to the driver's seat. "Toby!"

"Would we have taken the deal?" I asked.

"Toby."

"Should we be help—"

"Toby, they said they'd coordinate an army. That's not what this is."

"We could—"

"Toby," Emma snapped. "People like us don't get in the way of this kind of shit. We're collateral damage to Kris and Zoe." As Emma spoke, the sky roared with fire again. I caught the shadow of someone in the air, cutting across the sky. Was that?

The rag doll corpse flew across my vision and landed down the road. No. It hadn't been Zoe.

"See?" Emma insisted. "We'll talk to Rehsman and go to San Francisco ourselves. This isn't our fight."

I looked back at the hotel. Wasn't it? Wasn't it what we'd just been talking about? What we'd just—

"Toby. The keys."

I went to speak, and then I saw her.

Zoe stood in the air above the motel, cut against the moon. It almost looked like her eyes were glowing in the silver moonlight, but that was impossible. She... Emma was right. We didn't have an army, and this was so far beyond us.

All I'd wanted to do back in Crescent was help. All I wanted to do now was help.

"Toby," Emma snapped me out of it. I pulled open the car door, still staring at Zoe's silhouette in the moon. I felt the burning silver eyes on—

Wait, not on us.

Around us.

I felt my eyes widen at the realization. I wasn't seeing Zoe's eyes —that would have been impossible—but I was feeling her presence in the air. The force of her mind crackled against everything around us. A bubble surrounding Emma carved out the only safe space for what must have been miles.

Emma started the car once I was inside.

Fire roared across the skyline and I saw Kris, brilliant and orange, in the air. Zoe disappeared from her spot on the moon, flashing across the night sky with terrifying speed.

Emma pressed down on the gas.

Zoe waved a hand. I could see the edges of her fingernails glint in the firelight. Kris shattered into sparks.

Shingles tore off the motel as Emma peeled out of the parking lot. The roof's wood panels scattered to the wind next, followed by the walls and then buckling foundation and steel.

With a single wave of her hand, Zoe vaporized the place. It didn't seem like a joke anymore.

I felt my hands shaking.

Kris had been right. It had to be me and Emma. Nobody else could do this, but Emma was right, too. We'd need an army.

I watched Zoe floating over the ruined motel. I could only tell where she was in the dark night sky based on knowing where she'd been. As I stared, I felt her silver eyes wash over us again as she scanned the surrounding area. My vision stuttered momentarily as a blur washed over everything around us.

Zoe vibrated the air itself as we escaped into the night.

25

Zoe - Let The Flames Begin

That was the last distraction. The last of the extras that Kris and Lexi had brought along to their little honeymoon retreat. Now that they were gone, I could—

"Fight me, you bitch!" Kris snapped. Where had the suave man who was always in control gone? Where was the man who'd wished me a solemn goodbye before burning my fucking face off?

It didn't matter where his personality had gone; his body and power were right in front of me. That was all I needed for revenge, wasn't it?

A torrent of fire rushed at me, but I dropped to the ground before it was anywhere close. How had he felt so fast before? Was he just that sloppy now? Had I just been that weak when we'd fought last time? What a depressing thought, realizing that I'd been melted into the street because I didn't understand what I was working with. That I'd died screaming because I was scared of myself.

"Sure," I said as Kris flashed into sparks behind me, appearing in front of the edge of the growing wildfire he'd started. "Let's dance, Kris. I cleared the floor for us."

Kris lashed out, and another spiraling column of fire shot from his fingertips. I felt the searing heat wash against my face as it approached. It felt familiar, appropriate, like home. A breath before it hit me, just as it singed my hair, I rocketed to the side. Fire crashed where I'd been standing, turning that part of the parking lot into a temporary inferno.

Around us, the rest of the parking lot was a ruined battlefield, with burning cars, shattered glass, and the charred remains of the motel scattered everywhere.

I raised a hand and waved at one of the few vehicles I hadn't ruined in the first part of the evening. The black truck careened toward Kris, smashing into the pavement as he shattered into a brilliant shower of sparks.

With Lexi's shields, I couldn't feel him, but what I could feel was the fire roaring toward me. I shifted away, throwing and catching myself as the flames shot by.

"Is that all you have, Kris?" I asked. "All that power, and you just keep—" I stepped to the side, slipping fifty feet in a second to dodge a torrent of flame. "Throwing—" I tossed a shard of the hotel into the way as a blast rained from above. "Fire." The last attack was coming right for me. I made a point by simply waving my hand, whipping a roaring wave of air at the flames, scattering them to the wind.

Kris landed on the ground. He was panting already. He'd used up so much of his fire trying to pull my attention away from his little friends that he'd forgotten to take his time. At this rate, I wouldn't even need to find that Lexi girl. I'd let him exhaust himself, and then I could test the shield as much as I wanted.

Smoke billowed into the night sky, blending with the clouds and reflecting the orange glow of the flames in the seconds I offered him to speak.

"We were fighting for people like you, Zoe!" he yelled from his burning patch on the edge of what used to be a lawn. "For what they do to us."

"People like me?" I laughed. "You're nothing like me." I grabbed the same truck I'd thrown earlier, forcing Kris to blink away from it, reforming in other flames. He was trying to buy time by talking to me. All I had to do was keep him moving.

"For people like us," he repeated. He was behind me now. My mind spun my body so I could watch him. "What they do to us is inhumane. We're fighting for—" he shattered into sparks.

"I don't need you to fight for me."

"Them," he finished. He was on top of the battered and twisted motel sign now.

"Them?" I asked.

"People like Emma—"

This time, I cut him off, ripping the signage out from under him and sending it flying out into the sea. Kris didn't hit the ground, so he opened his mouth to speak.

But the sign never touched the water.

My mind wrapped around the remnants of the sign, ripping it backward across the sky. Just as Kris was standing up, it cracked against his spine. He flew through the air, soaring toward me. I reached out my hand, and he disappeared into another shower of sparks.

"Did I strike a nerve?" Kris asked. He was behind me again. The longer this went on, the more it felt like my only option was to exhaust him. He slipped away from everything, and even if I hit him, I would just bounce off the girl's shields.

I had to find her. She had to be nearby for her shields to stay wrapped around him. That was how their damned soul-pairing worked. She got to protect him from everything I had. How annoying.

I felt my power bristle at the idea of being denied.

How could I draw her out of hiding, though?

"You know she was here, right? Emma was here. She was making a deal with us about how to kill you."

"You're lying," I hissed. I pulled a tree out of the forest and sent it careening toward where his voice was coming from. I felt the heat as he flashed into existence in front of me, standing on the hood of a burning car. The cedar erupted into brilliant flames behind us.

"I'd let you read it out of me, but we both know I wouldn't survive that."

I flipped the car. He was gone. Then, back on the motel rubble, sitting this time. "I'm already going to kill you," I hissed. "Why lie to piss me off?"

"I'm not lying,"—Kris stood—"and maybe I'm just thinking about burning bridges. You know how it is with fire." Kris held up a hand, and flames licked at his fingertips. "Also..."

I felt overwhelming heat as the entire inferno that Kris had set up around us roared toward me, crashing in from every direction in a towering wall of fire that folded over us.

My cheek burned. I felt heat. It didn't feel like home this time. It felt like—I just had to charge through the flames. I could move fast enough that—

My power wasn't faltering, but my body was frozen, unwilling to issue a command. There was so much fire. I just had to—I just needed to—

My mind grabbed my wrist and tore it backward, tearing my arm from its socket and forcing my body to move, twisting in inhuman ways to follow the whims of my power. I shot off into the air, twisting and somersaulting until I crashed through the wall of fire.

My skin burned and bubbled. I felt the fire tear at me. I felt myself melting into the street. I felt the nothing of eternity. No. No.

No.

My twisting and broken arm righted me as I came out the other side of the flames. Before I had the chance to think, my power snapped it at the elbow, letting the arm twist in foreign ways. My fingers followed, shattering only to get righted by my mind, letting them snap and point at a thousand objects.

I hadn't realized it, but I was screaming. All at once, a hundred commands shot out into the air, grabbing every object around Kris and sending them seeking after him. My voice went hoarse.

Kris teleported away, and my shattered arm followed. He flashed above the parking lot, and the shards of glass, car, motel, and chunks of flesh kept on him. Several collided with him before he got away, this time knocking him off balance.

My scream faltered as I ran out of air, but my limp arm kept whipping after Kris, following his every move from my vantage point in the sky. He'd faltered. Then he'd found his footing. He'd try to counterattack. He'd get cut off.

My other arm snapped at the shoulder.

The ground itself rose to catch Kris, and I snagged his foot. A thousand missiles collided with him at once, each breaking against his shield until the first didn't.

A silver barrier shot up from the ground, and I saw her hidden in the tree line. I dove.

Kris screamed and turned into a shower of sparks.

I was fast, but teleportation was faster. Kris flashed in front of Lexi and summoned a wall of fire. I slammed on the brakes, stopping in midair. The wind following me carved a hole in Kris' flames.

Kris took something out of his pocket and clicked it. I couldn't tell what it was, but Lexi screamed as he pushed it into her chest, then turned into a shower of sparks.

I heard Kris behind me. He coughed. It was wet.

I felt static in the air, and there was a flash beside Lexi.

"NO!" she and I screamed it together.

The man was gone as soon as he'd flashed into existence, disappearing with Lexi.

Kris chuckled behind me, barely audible over the sound of the crackling fire. "Okay, Zoe, let's do—"

I cut him off by ripping the air around him away. I saw his body flicker, but the fire immediately went out. After a second, he gasped for breath, holding his hand out toward me. Fire wouldn't come out of it as long as I had his air. I flicked my head to the side and cracked his arm in a dozen places. He didn't have a shield anymore. I could control him. He was mine.

Kris used some of his last desperate air to scream, and I wrapped my mind around his chest, ratcheting up the pressure as each rib cracked. Kris half turned into fire but couldn't burn enough to teleport away.

"Like I said, we're not the same," I hissed. I walked up to him and pinned him to the pavement. He clawed at the cracked asphalt as he asphyxiated. "Power's a neat trick until I figure it out." Kris sputtered halfway into flames again but couldn't get the full way there.

I flipped the man over, forcing him to look up at me. The fire burning in his eyes now wasn't his power; it was raw hatred. "No," he choked. The words came out like they were fighting through acid. The cracks in his ribs and spirit must have been corroding his speech. "This isn't how it ends," he managed.

"Yeah,"—I put a foot on his chest—"it is."

Kris snapped his good arm onto my ankle, and I felt my skin bubble as he poured all the fire he had left into me. My mind strayed to the pain for a second, and Kris flashed away, landing further toward where the motel had been, close to the cliff side. He choked in air and stood.

I growled. I could feel my pant leg fused to my flesh.

"I'm not going out without you, Zoe—" He fired the last massive torrent, but my power smashed it to the side as I reached out and stole the air away again, but this time I snapped my power around his windpipe as well. He froze and coughed some of his precious oxygen out. His eyes were full of fury as I held him there. I watched it melt into panic and then slowly to regret.

The surrounding fires flared as he struggled against my hold, but he and I both knew it was useless. He was wasting his last seconds on Earth, raging against his fate. He managed to raise a hand, but the fire didn't answer his call.

"I'm sorry, Lex," he whispered. What a waste of his last breath.

I watched Kris writhe, and then I watched him hang limp in the air for a moment. My shattered arm drifted idly to my cheek, reopening the cuts I'd carved into it.

I turned away from his floating body, feeling the itching pain of my seared ankle and everything else that had gotten caught in the inferno. I took a deep breath. The night air was cool, but it tasted like smoke.

Kris was still floating where he'd choked. I could feel him.

I didn't want to feel him.

I wanted him gone.

My shattered arm reached backward, sending Kris' body flying off the edge of the cliff.

I flew away.

Kris scattered on the rocks.

26

Toby - The Last Moments

The plan had been to drive the rest of the way to San Francisco overnight, but once we'd gotten away from Zoe, the adrenaline came crashing down, and any ambitions we'd had to make it there faded into the background. Emma and I had gone to sleep in the truck, me in the front seat and her split between the back and trunk. Size-wise, the arrangement made no sense, but that was chivalry for you.

We'd gotten up in the early morning, or at least as early in the morning as we could manage. Our first attempt, getting up at dawn, had been just as ambitious as our driving plans. Neither happened. Staying locked in a tub together had been boring, but it'd somehow also been exhausting. Lying together in that damned place had left little pains all over our bodies…

Then there was everything we'd seen after. Was that the end of the Red? Were they gone? What was Zoe going to do if…

Kris had said that there were more of them out there than we understood. Even if that had been the end of Kris and Lexi, it wouldn't be the end of the Red or Zoe's rampage.

Emma had stepped out of the car to get some fresh air and then used the time to check the guns and magazines we'd stolen from the motel. She was meticulous about the process, which made sense. As far as I could tell, she was the same about most things in her life.

The only part missing right now was hygiene. Neither Emma nor

I had a chance to get clean after that motel room. I needed a good shower, but at this point, I would have settled for some gas station bottled water.

I poked around the car to watch Emma again as she reassembled Lexi's gun. She clicked each part into place with practiced ease. She clocked me watching after a moment and nodded for me to join her.

I complied, even though I didn't love where it was going.

Emma turned Lexi's gun to me again, offering the handle. She shook it insistently when I didn't accept, so I relented. "I'm gonna show you how to shoot," she said. Before I had time to express my feelings, she pushed back on them. "It's a useful skill, Toby. You should be ready to use one if you need to. It's all people like us have."

"I've seen you kick a lot of ass with just hands and fists," I pointed out.

"Okay. This is all people like us have that doesn't involve years of training," she said. I caught her frowning at the last part like she realized that learning to shoot a gun and being good with one were also separated by the aforementioned years of training. "Just work with me here, Toby."

I sighed. "What am I shooting at?"

Emma turned to the forest at the side of the highway, taking several steps down the bank and into the ditch past it. Once I'd joined her, she pointed at a fir tree about twenty feet away. It seemed like too close a target, but I wasn't about to question it.

I took a deep breath. "Why do I need to do this?" I asked.

"So you can shoot something," she said.

"I can stop time."

"You can stop time when it works," she corrected, "so we're making a backup plan here." Emma moved beside me and grabbed my right hand alongside the gun. She guided me into position. "Perfect form would have you spread your legs and ground yourself," she explained, "but I don't want you to focus on that. We're not target shooting."

"Aren't we?" I asked.

"We won't be," Emma corrected. She kept one hand on mine, and I felt the other in the small of my back, offering reassuring pressure. "We just need to get a shot off, center of mass. Nothing fancy."

I nodded.

Emma tightened her grip on my hand to stabilize it. "Stop shaking."

"You're right, I'm doing it intentionally," I said.

"Well, then stop," she responded, purposefully missing the sarcasm. I sighed and tried to hold my breath when she lined up the shot. I could feel her squeezing my trigger finger; I could feel her pressing in on me, training me how to kill and-

I flinched and fired.

"Dammit," she hissed as she pulled her hand off the gun. The gunshot echoed off the forest, cascading in different directions, but my target was unharmed. I shoved the gun back at Emma. She didn't accept it.

"I'm not going to shoot anyone," I said. "I'm not shooting a gun," I repeated.

"Really, after all of this, this is how I hit an impasse with my soulmate?" she asked. "Not the war we started, but the gun shooting?" Emma pressed the gun back into my chest. I wasn't going to win an argument over that because the soulmate point really wasn't fair. I hadn't used it yet, but when I did, it would be for something monumental, like the color of the curtains. I pointed the gun back toward the tree before she instructed me to.

"There we go," she said. "You've got this."

"I don't like it," I said before pulling the trigger. I'd be verbally defiant, if nothing else.

Emma stared into the forest for a moment and then hung her head. "Well, you're not a crack shot."

"Did you think I would be?"

"I was hoping your power would help," she said.

"I can see the target," I affirmed.

"Now hit it."

I pulled the trigger again, and the gun practically leapt from my hands. There was a distinct lack of splintered bark in the woods.

"Maybe something automatic?" Emma sighed.

"Automatic?"

"You pull the trigger once and fire tons of bullets." That sounded like something from a movie. "There aren't many of them left. We had them before the plague, but they're all antiques now."

"You want me to fire an antique?" I asked.

"If it'll get you to hit the target," Emma said.

That was fair. I nodded along with her point and drew the gun up again. If I kept missing, it was going to look like false incompetence. How hard was it to hit a tree? It wasn't like it was swaying; I was aiming for the damned base.

"Think you've got it this time?" she asked. "Just jumpy, eh?" she continued. I appreciated her trying to be more positive, but I wasn't sure I loved how obvious the attempt was.

"I mean, isn't everyone jumpy their first time?"

"I wasn't," she pointed out. Emma reached over and grabbed the gun from me. "Just watch, okay? Watch my form and breathing and—" She pulled the trigger twice to cut herself off. Bullets splintered the bark.

The sound faded, and I checked her shot. The marks were less than an inch apart.

"Damn."

"That's easy," Emma said, "it's easy. You just need to get used to it. Want to try again?"

"Am I allowed to say no?" I asked.

"Only two shots left in this magazine. We can wrap up after that."

I sighed and took the gun back, staring at it.

Emma pulled hers out of her holster.

"Joining me?" I asked.

"Someone needs to hit the tree," she said, "and I missed this. Target shooting."

"Really?"

"It's cathartic, like reading or writing."

"You write?" I asked.

"I wrote." She leveled her gun.

"Past tense?"

"Mhm."

"What'd you write?" I asked. She answered my question by firing her gun. The tree splintered again in the same spot. Sap welled. "Poetry back in the day," she finished.

"And you stopped?" I asked.

"Yeah, I was self-aware enough to realize it sucked," she pointed out, "so I stuck to reading it, and—" She fired again. Poor tree. "I learned to shoot. Found out it was more my speed. Between this and reading, I can get the stress out."

"That's not a normal combination of things to relax," I said.

"Sure, a lot of people read."

I went to correct her until I saw her smile. She was grinning, waiting for me to give her the satisfaction. I held my tongue for a moment. Then, "I didn't mean the reading."

"I know," Emma said. She smiled but obviously understood that I'd caught and fed her the joke. After a second, she spoke up. "Do you wanna try again?"

I shook my head, and she sighed. "Can't we just stick to this being cathartic for you?" I asked.

Emma answered by emptying the rest of her magazine into the woods. Even with her careful control, some shots missed the tree. I saw her shoulders relax as the echoing crack of the gunshots faded into the canopy. Once there had been quiet, the first brave birds resumed chirping. Emma was still staring off into the woods.

I took the magazine out of Lexi's gun—I'd seen Emma do it three times earlier—and walked over to Emma. Her stare was distant. I rested a cautious hand on her shoulder instead of saying her name.

"I've known her since she was like this big." She moved her hand several times before finding the right height to show me. It took a moment, but I caught she was talking about Zoe, who apparently hadn't grown much in the past years. "They gave her to me and told me to take care of her, but now—" a single sob escaped as a cough. Emma tried to choke it down.

I squeezed her shoulder.

"Now look at it. This is what we've come to. I left her behind, and now we have to kill her."

"You didn't leave her behind," I said.

"Do you know why I had to take her in?" she asked. It was off-topic, but I shook my head. "When she was twelve and just learning how strong she was, she accidentally killed her parents," she said. "It wasn't even her fault. She just didn't know how to control herself so—" Another squeaking sob. "So they gave her to me, Toby. Another girl with no parents. I reigned in her powers. It was perfect. We've been together ever—"

"Emma."

She took a deep breath. "I have to do this," she said after she steeled herself. "It needs to be us. I have to give her peace." She stared out at the sap dripping down from our target tree.

"Emma..."

"Let's go, Toby."

27

Toby - Deals and Devils

Of all the things we'd expected to find in the middle of the highway, one of our worst enemies wasn't one of them.

First, we'd assumed that after last night, Lexi was likely dead. Second, we didn't know how or why she was in the middle of the road waiting for us with a barrier up. The answer was that she'd been teleported here by the same man who had saved her last night. That was two for the price of one.

As for why she was here, she was surrendering and trying to reopen the conversation.

Lexi had complied thus far, which was why I actually considered it when she looked up at us from her seat in the open trunk and asked, "Are the cuffs necessary?" She looked down at them. "And weren't these ours?"

"You're a wanted criminal," Emma said. "I'm part of the DPR. The cuffs stay on, be glad it isn't worse."

A car shot by, heading down the forest highway and ignoring the handcuffed woman in a tense conversation on the side of the road. The smell of pine and damp earth from the recent rain filled the air. The scenery was certainly more pleasant than the collective mood.

"Are you part of the DPR? Does your office exist anymore?" Lexi asked. She caught my eye as she did. Hopefully, she understood I was telling her to back off.

"Think I get to figure that out later," Emma answered. She was leaning against the side of the truck, partially in the dent Zoe had made last night, picking at her cuticles. She wasn't taking any skin off, almost strumming like a guitar. Just another entry in her long line of tics. "Mind explaining what the hell you're doing here? Thought shit was over for you."

"Again?"

"I'm waiting for an honest answer," Emma spat.

"She's been telling the truth so far," I pointed out. Emma tsked at my response but didn't grace it with words. "At least far as I can tell."

"I said I was here to help you. Don't know how many ways you want me to say that. Spent the time to find you, didn't I? Stranded myself out here."

"You've all managed that a couple of times, and it's never gone well." Emma had stunning control over her tone, so I was probably the only person who could read the open hostility in it. Then again, maybe I was just giving her too much credit. She continued, "Why should I buy that? Now you're here out of altruism?"

"Kris is dead," Lexi said. Flat. Almost catatonic.

"What?" I asked before Emma had a chance to speak. I'd assumed that, if she'd been able to get out, then Kris certainly could have.

"He stayed behind after he called our teleporting friend in to grab me. She was going to kill me, but—as soon as I was gone, he didn't have the shield. I want to think he put up a fight, but..."

"I'm sorry," I said.

"You're sure?" Emma cut in. It was my turn to shoot her a look, but she was mid interview, attention locked on Lexi instead of me.

"You'd know if he died too," Lexi answered, nodding in my direction. "So, now I'm here because I want to help you."

"Help us with what?" Emma asked.

"Your Zoe problem."

"Zoe's not–" Emma went to snap at Lexi but bit back the words. There wasn't a point in lying about it. She just didn't enjoy being on the same page as the girl. "Why would we need your help? All you guys do is die to her."

"She wants to kill me the most out of anyone," Lexi said. "I'm our best chance of drawing her out. Picking a fight where we have a chance."

"If she wanted you dead, she would have found you by now," I said.

"Zoe can't see Lexi under the shields, so she can't find her as long as she has one up and…" Emma motioned to the woman. The silver outline around Lexi was obvious enough to me, but I was impressed that Emma noticed it. "Same thing as her not being able to track us as long as we're together."

"She's not trying to kill you, at least," Lexi said. "But yes, that's the truth. I am here to try to remake the pitch—"

"So what," Emma started, "you wanna fight her? We can make that happen. I can stop holding back and shut down that shield for you. I didn't think losing Kris would make you suicidal."

"Emma." I cut her off.

"What? It's true," Emma pointed out as she turned to me. Lexi rolled her eyes from the trunk. "She'll be a splatter on the sidewalk before she even sees Zoe."

"She's tried that. Multiple times."

"She won't fuck it up again,"—Emma turned back to Lexi—"and if you're so eager to die fighting her, just go do it. Don't get us involved in your bullshit like we're suddenly friends. You lost your leverage with Kris."

"Just a second. Emma," I stepped in, literally, just one pace closer to Emma to draw her attention over to me. "We should at least hear her out. She's just as wrapped up in this as we are. We were listening before."

"Just as in it as we are?" she repeated. "You're kidding, right? She's the whole reason we're here. None of this would have happened if—"

"If we hadn't met," I finished for her.

Emma opened her mouth to say something, then looked away

instead, staring at the forest for a moment longer than the natural silence should have lasted. "Fucking hell," she sighed. "You two talk about it. I'll be somewhere else on the fucking highway, I guess." She didn't throw another insult at Lexi as she took her first steps off the side of the road and toward the woods. I just hoped she wasn't going to shoot the trees again.

Though, the stress relief might have been productive. She was angry and passionate, but it felt like it was more about the world than this conversation.

Once Emma had walked away, I walked to the front seat and grabbed the key to the handcuffs from the cup holder. Lexi watched as I came back around the car and palmed it.

She waited for a second, giving me a chance to let her go. Then spoke. "Quite the charmer you have there."

"She is a charmer, thanks," I said, crossing my arms. "And I would have said the same about you and Kris." Lexi's eyes jumped around my face, trying to figure out how much I was willing to continue banter with her, but I didn't even know myself. She settled on staying quiet.

"I'm sorry about Kris," I said.

"No, you're not."

"I can be sympathetic without liking him," I pointed out. There was more I could say there, like that I was being accused of not mourning a man who'd tried to kidnap me, of not lamenting the man who'd started all this, but I didn't. "I'm sorry for you."

It took a moment. "Thanks, I guess." She took a deep breath, and I couldn't tell whether she was steeling herself or sighing. "I'll deal with it later. If there is a later."

"Focus on the now, then?" I asked. I opened my hand to show her the key, even though I understood she'd already seen me grab it.

Lexi nodded.

"Before I unlock these. What's the plan?"

"Reds have my back on this. That's the plan."

"Pardon?"

"Everyone's in," Lexi said. "Look, not everyone has seen her in action yet, but they can figure out what's coming. She came for me in the middle of the city. She tore a motel apart for Kris. Zoe's going to keep coming for us until nobody's left. It was why Kris pushed me so hard on your offer."

I didn't comment, so she continued.

"Who knows what happens once she's out of members to kill? She's already caused enough collateral."

"More?" I asked.

"Zoe's been busy," she said, "not everything's as flashy as fighting Kris or myself but... If the news wants to keep the coverup going, they're gonna be reporting a lot of gas leaks over the past few days." She frowned. "Lord knows how they'll explain the cars half a click from the freeway."

"Shit."

"Yeah. That about sums it up." Lexi held out the handcuffs again, letting them jingle. I considered but didn't move to undo them. "Look, Kris' whole point was that we could handle our own shit. That the government didn't need to regulate everyone over Upsilon to keep things moving. It's supposed to be self-correcting."

"Going well right now."

She frowned at the shot but didn't refute it. "Look, Kris had people on his side for a reason. They know Zoe's coming for them, and they're willing to go after her first, if it means they can prove his point." She must have seen the question on my face, because she stopped the monologue and waited for me to ask it.

"You keep saying Kris' instead of 'ours.'"

"I believed in Kris. His vision was his. I couldn't give a damn about the DPR or that bullshit as long as they leave me alone, which they were before. I wasn't worth their attention because the scale's stupid." She sighed. They were almost constant in the conversation, littered between words, but this one stood out. "I was his. He was mine. I'm going to finish what he started. Or die trying."

I tried to find the words, but she affirmed the point for me.

"Yeah, I know, probably the latter." Lexi let her hands fall, leaving the handcuffs in her lap. "If I can help take—shut her down. Then I have to do it, don't I? What's the other option? Watch my soulmate's dream fall apart in front of me and let everyone I've known for the past years get crushed one by one while I hide behind a shield?"

There wasn't anything to say at this point. I moved the key out of my palm to use it, but she continued before I'd freed her.

"I'm not growing old with him, but I can at least do right by him. Do the right thing. Save some people on the way. Hell, maybe I live through it with all that shit you have going on."

"Wouldn't count on it," I said as I clicked the handcuffs open. She'd been too far into her thoughts to notice me undoing them, but she rubbed her wrists all the same.

"And I'll turn myself in after if you two still want that as part of the deal. Hell, everyone I asked agreed to as long as it gets them through this."

"You were the one against it before."

"I wasn't going to let Kris' dream die so he could buy me some extra protection," she sighed. "Look where that got us, though."

"Well, I'm willing to hear you out, at least."

"Isn't that kind?"

"Maybe we just really need extra bodies, and you were the first offer?"

"Maybe you saw Zoe last evening."

I nodded along with that.

"Can it be my turn to ask a question?" Lexi was still rubbing her wrists but had them together like the cuffs were still on. "What the fuck is the DPR doing about all this? Zoe's been on a rampage and—"

"That's a great question, and if I knew, I'd tell you," Emma said as she rejoined the conversation. "Far as we can tell, Rehsman has the same plan as you."

"They're going to—"

Emma chuckled. "No, his plan seems to be that you're gonna take care of Zoe for him. Two birds, one stone. His plan is for you to try your plan."

I turned to Emma.

"Why lose his people when she's doing his job for him right now?" Emma asked once neither of us spoke.

"So he's following Kris' doctrine," Lexi half-laughed. "What a fucking joke."

"Seems like," Emma said, "but we're not really on speaking terms until we solve the other half of the problem."

"You're wiped from the database," Lexi sighed. "Fuck it. Take everything you want from us."

Emma crossed her arms and made a note of Lexi's unfastened handcuffs, but didn't say anything about it.

"What was that?" I asked.

"We'll wipe you from the database when we're done." I caught it as she spoke, the way her voice rose at the end.

"Emma, a second, please." I pulled Emma away from the car, just out of Lexi's earshot if we were whispering. During the entire walk, my soulmate questioned what the hell I was doing with her eyes. "I think they've already done it," I said.

"What?"

"When she was talking about wiping us from the database," I said. "She slipped up the first time, and the second time, she was forcing the lie when she'd said 'after we're done.'"

"Are you sure?"

"I think they wanted to accept our deal last night. In fact, I think they did," I said, "and then Zoe interrupted before they could pass that on."

"So we could just leave," Emma said. She looked at the dirt before I did. Her brow furrowed. Some of the last remnants of day-old makeup cracked almost imperceptibly. "But—" She swore. "Now I'm choosing to do it if we work with them. If we're right."

"I know," I said.

"Toby, I—we still have to help her and—"

I rested my hand on her shoulder and squeezed, then brushed

her hair back behind her ear before resetting it for her. "Emma."

"I wanted to be forced," she said.

"You said it yourself. Doing what you have to do doesn't make you a worse person."

"I feel worse saying it, but—"

"Then I will," I said before turning to Lexi and raising my voice. "Lex, let's finish this."

"Hope it's a good ending," Lexi said.

I nodded. It was never going to be happy, but it could at least be right.

28

Toby - Wildfire I

If I was going to die today, this was the place where it was going to happen.

Lexi hadn't given us time after agreeing to their plan. Every minute we waited, Zoe could track down and kill another one of their the Red. Eventually, there wouldn't be enough of them left to challenge her.

It was happening, and it was happening today.

The skeletons of half-finished houses lined the dirt roads we were waiting on, their frames exposed and bare. Piles of lumber and stone lay scattered, providing potential hiding spots but also potential projectiles.

The under-construction suburb between Crescent and Arcata felt like a compromise. There wasn't anywhere that you wanted to fight Zoe, but if you were looking for unpopulated, then your options were this or an open field.

Both, when you thought about them, felt like suicide, but this at least had some cover, which was reassuring...if possibly useless.

I had Todd's glacial old phone in my hand, sending a last message to him and then to Mom and Dad.

Hey! I'm Using Todd's phone. I broke mine. I just wanted to say I love you. Things are going well with the new girl.

Emma was reading over my shoulder. "New girl? They know about me?"

"My mom sussed out that I was dating someone when she called about the job." I sent the text and shoved the phone into my pocket. "Doesn't know the rest of it, though."

"We'll tell her when we visit," Emma said. I smiled at that, but it almost felt like we were dancing on the edge of oversweet, like the police officer who said he was one day away from retirement.

Depending on how Emma treated getting erased from the database, she was essentially one day away from retirement.

The air filled with static again, and another Red flashed into existence. The teleporter the Red had access to had spent the better part of the last hour flitting back and forth, carrying one volunteer at a time. Each new arrival brought a new wave of tension, like a second hand ticking toward doomsday.

It was impressive that they had a teleporter at all. They were rare, but of course, it was nothing compared to Rehsman. I supposed that Rehsman not showing up here was his last retreat from the conflict. Emma was right. He hadn't cared. Some of us would live, and some of us would die. As far as the DPR was concerned, it was all victories.

It made you understand why something like the Red existed in the first place. How that kind of sentiment could build. How the pinpricks dancing on the inside of my skin could drive me to join any fight I was called to.

Zoe's dissertation was sitting on my coffee table back in my apartment. I had to read it if—when we got home.

Emma rested a hand on my shoulder. "Are you ready for this?"

I chuckled at the idea of that. "No."

"Good," she said. It was quiet, solemn. "We shouldn't be." Emma sighed. "I don't think this is something we should ever be ready for."

"But—"

"But I..." There was a pointed pause. "We have to do this. It has to be—" Emma stopped before choosing whether she was going to say 'me' or 'us.' I didn't force her to make that choice.

The breeze rustled through the plastic sheeting on some of the half-finished homes, adding to the quiet whispers of the Red around us. The sun disappeared behind the clouds, and it didn't look like it was coming back.

Lexi stood on one of the front steps of the houses. Everyone must have been here.

The girl took a deep breath. She was too young to be up there, and the space beside her looked empty without Kris. Was that what it was like? Was that what would happen if Emma or I died today? Would we have to walk through life with a shadow of the other person missing at our side?

Lexi took a deep breath and then spoke. It wasn't the catatonic tone she'd used when talking about Kris or the hate she'd used for Zoe. After everything, it was just a voice. A girl in over her head.

"We're here for one reason," she started. "And it's not fear. We are only the targets of that monster because we were the ones brave enough to stand up to everything they did. We were the ones who heard Kris' dream of a world where we protect each other, and we were the ones willing to fight for it."

I held Emma's hand.

"The DPR isn't here. They're scared. They've failed each and every person in and around Crescent City."

Emma's nails dug into my palm.

"Well. We won't. Every one of us who wakes up tomorrow will wake up a hero, and everyone who dies will be buried a martyr. We don't need to fight the whole system. We just need to kill one monster, and we'll have proven our point better than any plan we could have dreamed of!"

There were scattered cheers that echoed off the house frames. She was doing a good job of making them sound like the heroes in all this, but then again, she had a captive audience.

"They told us we could never stand up to the Department, and now they've been telling us that we're all going to die."

I squeezed Emma's hand as the pressure grew. This was it.

"Well, we're not going to listen. Today, we control our own destiny. If we're fated to die, it's time to fight against fate!"

As Lexi said the last words, she dropped her shield.

29

Zoe - Wildfire II

I staggered into the office space I'd claimed over the last day, my shirt and jacket stained with fresh blood. As I pressed open the door, I stumbled again and hacked. More blood poured onto my clothes as I vomited it onto the floor.

What was going on? I hadn't gotten hit. The last of the bastards I'd visited hadn't even seen me before I'd smashed him into paste. Why was this happening? Why was—

My power cracked against the door frame as I walked through. I was taking too many breaks. I couldn't hunt when I was getting healed, but I kept needing attention.

I'd tried staying out there. I'd tried finding a healer nearby instead of coming all the way back to Crescent, but they weren't strong enough. The boy I'd found. He was the perfect one, the only one powerful enough to keep up with my—our mission.

Once I was in the main office I saw him, half-conscious on the floor, his wrist pinned to the wall by a radiator I'd twisted into handcuffs. He scrambled on the floor as I approached, his shoes squeaking against the cracked tile.

Why was he so jumpy? Why was he so jittery? What was he so afraid of? I'd come back here so many times. I'd been here over and over and I was never anything but nice. I was never anything but—

My power crashed through one of the tiles on the ceiling and he startled to attention. Dust and plaster rained down on the pair of us as I waved a hand and the radiator freed him.

The boy backed into the corner. I cocked my head, and he slid over despite still trying to walk away. "I don't think you're keeping up," I said. "I still have so much work to do and—" I chuckled, and the laughter turned into sputtering wet coughs. "I don't think I can do it like this."

He looked me up and down, still trying to walk away despite it clearly getting him nowhere. My power hissed around his wrist and pulled his hand to my chest.

Once again, no cooling relief. I glared at the glassy eyes of the boy and he seemed to return to the present. He swallowed, and I felt his power flow through me before I had to threaten him. He was learning. He was understanding. He knew that I was in the right here. He understood I was the hammer of justice and—

I coughed again. Blood poured from my mouth and coated his arm. He closed his eyes, and I felt the pressure of his healing build, his power twisting inside me.

I heard his words in my head. He didn't know if he could fix it, but he understood that he needed to. He wanted to take his time, but I didn't have time I—

My power spoke up in the background. There was a new name on the radar. Someone who I desperately wanted to see. Lexi had dropped her shield. "You cocky bitch," I snapped. The boy healing me jumped, but didn't stop. He knew better than that. I felt the laughter rise in my throat. This was my chance. I would finally take her down. Complete the fucking set.

My power clawed on the outer brickwork of the abandoned office building, first tearing out the bricks and then pulling at the steel below it. I wanted to go. I needed to go. WE wanted to go. How long was she going to keep the shield down? I couldn't wait. "Hurry up!" I snapped. The boy flinched as much as he could while locked in place by my power.

My mind pulled at the side of the building, digging deeper and deeper, like a car tearing apart the mud while stuck in park.

I couldn't wait.

We couldn't wait.

The boy flinched again, and I snapped him rigid.

I didn't have time for this.

"Fine, you're coming with me," I hissed. Before the boy could say anything, we were out in the sky. The cold air cut through my blood-soaked clothes, stinging my skin. Below us, the city blurred into a tapestry of glowing dots.

She had no idea what she'd done by calling me.

30
Toby - Wildfire III

The shock wave came before any sound did. It was like standing in one of those demolition disaster movies, where houses were swept away like the breeze. It was surreal power. I felt it hum under my feet, picking me up off the ground. There was a half-second where everything felt calm.

A shimmering barrier snapped in front of Emma and me as the half-finished homes shattered into splinters and shrapnel, tearing across the group we'd assembled. Lexi held as much as she could back, lumber and stone crashing against her barriers.

Some people were lost between the barriers. They vanished into the whipping wind, thrown a hundred feet by the shockwave of Zoe's arrival.

Dust and debris floated down in the aftermath of the shock wave, but some of it didn't. Chunks of timber and concrete piping were stuck permanently suspended animation.

I dropped low as a second crack echoed across the sky, and each piece of the construction site around us lashed out again, either crashing against Lexi's shields or flying off into the distance.

A third shock wave. A fourth. The dust kicked up by the assault became blinding, limiting visibility and outlining each of the Red as silhouettes to each other. Lexi screamed.

We needed Zoe to come close. I couldn't see her, but if she just hit us from a mile away, there was nothing Emma and I could do to stop her.

A sonic boom cracked across the sky, rattling piles of fractured lumber and shaking eardrums. I managed to cover my ears, so my vision only stuttered for a moment.

A silhouette in the sky, high above us.

I was just about to shout out her position when I heard what remained of the house closest to me groan. Emma snatched me by the collar, and we ran as the foundation tore itself from the earth, spraying dust, clay, and stone into the air.

Was this better than having given her a perfect line of sight on us? Should we have been in the open field?

No, we knew it from the start. Fighting Zoe anywhere was suicide.

"Up high!" I finally managed through the steps Emma was pulling me on. I couldn't see the Red around me, but I heard them react.

A massive beam of lumber flew through the sky, following the sound of my voice. Another shimmering shield flashed in front of Emma and me. It dissipated a second later, Lexi's attention pulled by another projectile, another blast, another.

What the fuck were we going to do? Emma needed to see Zoe and be close, or I needed her on the ground to do anything with my power. By the time that happened, we'd all be fucking mulch.

Then, my call paid off. Something cracked through the sky; a purple shimmering beam shot out of the smoke. Zoe dove out of the way.

Then there was another attack.

Then another.

But none of them could hit her. Even when some looked like they made purchase, I could tell through the clearing dust that the shots were shattering inches from her skin.

What the attacks were doing was keeping her distracted. Zoe weaved between the strikes, but she'd stopped fighting back in the same way. Or at least it wasn't as devastating. Her pointed retaliations weren't knocking all of us to our knees.

Emma and I had a chance to find our footing.

Zoe screamed, and then I heard a single word echo through the entire construction site in some twisted version of her voice.

"Enough."

Zoe slammed down to the ground, and the world shook. The ground slid out from under me, tearing itself from under my feet. I toppled to the dirt. Emma landed beside me, digging into the overturned earth with her nails as she did.

My face was still buried in the earth, but I could feel the silver eyes Zoe'd had back at the motel falling around us. Shit.

"Emma!" I pulled her from the ground, ripping her up and helping her steady herself as the surrounding air blurred, vibrating and distorting the light.

The silver eyes somehow saw past Emma and stared at me.

Emma threw out her hand.

The air cleared and Zoe dropped to the ground, stumbling, suddenly asked to use her feet instead of her mind. Emma had—

Oh shit.

Emma's eyes fluttered for a moment as she struggled against Zoe. I tried to pull out the gun she'd given me in time, but—

A stone flew at Zoe, slamming into her chest. A man sped up to her, carrying a blade.

Emma dropped.

The man who'd run up to Zoe twisted and writhed. Then popped.

Another shot, the same purple beam from before, erupted from the rubble, slamming into Zoe as she stumbled back in the air. The telepath sputtered, vomiting blood onto her jacket as she rose back into the air.

I turned my attention to Emma. I put my hand on her chest and felt it rise and fall, inconsistent but certainly alive. "Great job," I said as I got an arm under her. Zoe was in the air again. And who knew how much time Emma had bought us but—

One of the last few structures to our right creaked, and I heard the sound of snapping wood.

Emma pulled herself away from me. Pushing me to the other side of the column as it crashed down to the earth. We were both thrown in opposite directions.

Above us, Zoe coughed again and growled in frustration. She took off like a shot, cracking the air with another sonic boom but only arcing several hundred feet across the construction site to one of the completed homes on the edge.

The boom washed over me when my hands were still splayed by getting knocked over, and I screamed. The ringing took over, and my vision wobbled.

I saw Emma on the other side of the fallen lumber. Blood was starting to drip down from a cut on her forehead. She looked at me and then looked at Zoe's path.

No.

She'd kept saying that she was going to do this alone.

I saw her mouth sorry as she ran after Zoe, and I struggled to find balance from nothing.

Oh God.

31

Zoe - Die For You

I held the boy in place, but I heard his thoughts and saw the defiance in his eyes before he spoke. "No. You're hurting too many people."

My power snapped from his wrist to his neck, coiling around his throat and then shoving him. The drywall caved in as he smashed into it. He didn't have the air to gasp from the impact. His gaze softened for a second.

"Just do your damned job." I spat. I'd been sloppy out there. My legs were already weak.

He was quiet for too long. He was thinking about his parents, his work, what I was doing out th—

"Just one more time," I lied to cut off the thought. "You can go back to your mom. Clock in tomorrow." I approached, loosening my grip on him as I did. It took more effort than it should have, like I was tensing by letting go.

He looked down, avoiding my eyes. I placed his palm on my sternum.

"Just like that. Then it's all over." I pressed his hand harder against me, forcing his nails to dig into my skin through my torn and blood-soaked jacket.

"N—" The word trapped in his throat with a gurgle as his windpipe slammed shut. I staggered back a second before I realized what I'd done. With one more gurgle, the body slumped into the indent it had made in the drywall. Blood dripped from the edges of his lips.

"Fuck. Fuck. FUCK." I smashed the corpse through the wall, and it cracked against one of the supporting beams hidden inside. The house shook. "We needed him. Why would I do that? We—I—I—" I stumbled backward again, this time losing my footing, only catching myself a breath before I hit the ground.

With my options gone, exhaustion washed over me like a wave. How long could I keep going like this? I felt blood bubbling in my throat. How much did I have left?

I just needed a minute. I just needed more time to...

Fuck.

I could win this, and I had to. They were so close to running away. I was so close to the end. I could stop once they were all dead. Once I knew they were dead, I would...

No. I wouldn't get control once they were all dead. I had control right now, didn't I? This was what I wanted. This was what I'd wanted the whole time. I'd spent years holding back. Wasting my powers while vermin like Kris festered in the cracks of society. It'd just taken me dying to see that.

My forehead twinged. Where did this end? That wasn't how I did things before. That wasn't how... I just needed a minute.

I tried to push myself off the floor, but my power wasn't there to catch me. My body didn't have the strength left. I needed my mind to do the heavy lifting, but it wasn't there, and... It was because I wasn't being the hunter right now. I was getting hunted, but even then...beyond that.

It took that moment of confusion to realize that I couldn't feel the world around me. Instead of touching every inch of the room with my mind, I was alone in it. The only feedback I got was in my palms.

"Emma." I almost didn't recognize the way I said her name. It was venomous. Wrong. We were supposed to be together until the end. She was the person who'd saved me before, and now...

I turned, and there she was in the doorway, dried blood mixed with wet on the right side of her face, and her hair matted along with it. She said nothing, so I spoke first.

"Which one of them did that to you?"

"You," she answered. Her tone was flat, almost catatonic. "This stops now."

"I didn't do that,"—I tried to pick myself up off the ground again but didn't make it much further this time—"and if I did, you shouldn't have been in my way."

"Everyone's been in your way, Zoe."

"All your new fuckin' friends, I guess." I gave up on pushing off the ground and staggered to my feet. I was slow. Vulnerable. A thousand bruises added up as my power-starved me. "Here to say sorry? Maybe let me do my job?"

"Zoe..."

I lashed out, reaching at her and throwing what mental weight I had toward her chest. It splashed against her like a breeze, barely adjusting her collar. That had been everything I had. Why hadn't she fu—"I'm sorry. I'm sorry. I shouldn't have done that."

It took Emma a moment and a deep breath, her hand resting on her holster. "I can't let you keep hurting people," she said. "You're not going to stop."

"Emma. I can fix this. Once I've gotten rid of them. This is all their fault. Then I can keep you, and protect Toby and we—" She wasn't listening. "Fuck you then. You're just gonna stand there and judge me? I'm the one here trying to make things better."

"Who's them, Zoe?" Emma asked.

"There's a list," I lied. If I kept saying the names, I'd remember it, but people kept jumping on there. One after another. Another threat I needed to take care of. Another roadblock between me and the end of... whatever this had become.

"Where am I on it?"

I didn't have the answer to that, but my power flared in the back of my head. It knew exactly where she was. Climbing right to the top as long as she was in front of me. But...No. No, that was wrong. We'd spared Emma before. She hadn't done this to me. She hadn't—

She'd been my leash for so many years. Did that mean she needed to be on the list? Did that mean—

"Yeah," Emma said, disappointment dripping in her voice. "I thought so."

When she'd walked into the room, it'd been with careful steps. She'd been considering whether she wanted to do it, but now? At this moment? Emma was resolute.

So this was what it had come down to. I almost hadn't wanted to believe that voice when it whispered that everyone was against me, but... Of course, I should have been listening to it; it was me. The evening breeze had given way to rain behind me.

Emma's hand twitched. I lashed out, throwing my mind behind a wave of force. Emma's aura ate away at my strike, inch by inch, tearing it apart until it washed against her, just barely knocking her hip.

No. I was stronger than that. I was—

Emma rushed me down before I had the chance to strike again. Everything hurt. I felt the voice, my partner, burn away as Emma crossed the last inches.

There was no fancy form, no years of training, just a haymaker. Emma's fist slammed into my nose, snapping my head back and sending me reeling. I tried to raise a hand to stop her, but she slapped it back down. My power burned against the floor as she grabbed me by the collar, and then I felt her shin smash into my knee. The already weak leg buckled, and I dropped to the floor.

Emma kicked again, this time knocking me over onto the ground. I landed face-down against the splintered hardwood of the room. There was blood on the floor. I knew it was mine.

I heard the telltale click of Emma's holster behind me. "I'm sorry, Zoe."

I didn't have time for a response. My power flared, pushing through Emma's aura's acidic burn. I wrapped it around her wrist first, but it kept sliding off her skin, like contact with her melted my focus.

Instead of focusing, I raged.

The room whipped into a fury, and a wave of force slammed into Emma from the side. She flew to the left, sliding to a stop on the floor of the broken office, landing just short of the splintered desk. I tried to call for more force, more fury, but it wasn't there.

It wasn't Emma's power burning it away. It was the dread and regret in her eyes as she climbed back to her feet.

She was on top of me again, dashing across shards of wood and drywall to cross the gap. I tried to get a hand up to resist her, but I wasn't fast enough. Her boot smashed into my hand on the floor, dropping my support and letting me almost smash into the hardwood again.

My power caught me, but that meant it wasn't focused on her. Emma jumped on top of me. Her knees pinning my elbows to the floor. I screamed, and I couldn't hear whether there was more anger or pain in it. The tears in Emma's eyes shone in the early evening light as the rain started to blow into the office. She wound her fist.

I closed my eyes just before impact and felt my head slam against the hardwood before I felt the pain in my nose. I braced for a second, but...

I opened my eyes. Emma was breathing heavily on top of me, her chest heaving, her teeth gritted. She had her fist pulled back but was stuck there, frozen. "Please, Zoe," she whispered.

How had it come to this? How had I never seen that it was coming to this?

Emma dropped her wound punch and snatched the gun off her hip instead. She held it steady in place, trained between my eyes.

I reached up to grab the gun, and I managed to. Emma didn't pull away, but—

I held the gun in place, keeping it trained on my forehead. If anything, I was reassuring the shaking out of her wrists. What was I doing? What was this? I was going to die. She was going to kill me. Why wasn't I fighting back? All I had to do was—

She adjusted her grip on the gun again. I watched her bite her lip and shift her weight. My traitor hand held her steady.

Why was I so resigned? Why did—

A sob broke out of Emma. She dropped the gun, letting it clatter to the floor beside me.

In all our years together, I'd never been able to hear Emma's thoughts, but as she let go of the gun and my power came rushing back, I heard her.

I can't. I'm sorry, Zoe.

I screamed, and Emma snapped back to reality, trying to keep me pinned to the floor. My mind slammed into her chest, but it washed past her. So I hit again.

Nothing.

And again.

Nothing.

And again.

The third burned through everything she had, sending her soaring across the room. Emma cracked against the drywall and slumped down to the floor. Now that she was further away, I could pick myself off the hardwood.

I walked over to Emma on the ground. She struggled to get up, but she was still dazed. I held out a hand. But— Why had she hesitated? She'd been trying to kill me. She was right. She was on the list. I just had to—

I shook my head. She'd bought herself more time with that little stunt. I'd deal with her once I was finished with everyone else. That would be my debt repaid.

32

Toby - Splitting Seconds

I took a few seconds for a deep breath before searching in the pocket of my jacket for the knife Zoe had given me at the start of this. Emma told me to use the gun, but I wasn't sure how it would work in the time stop, and this felt... appropriate. Maybe too personal, but appropriate.

Emma was frozen in the corner of the room, looking like she'd just staggered to her feet after getting knocked over. There was blood and a broken wall from someone I didn't recognize. The furniture had all been pounded to mulch.

I turned to Zoe in the center of the room and took another deep breath. It was time to do what I had to.

Zoe blinked.

I jumped back toward the door and pressed myself against the wall. I could hear her on the other side, the evident confusion in her first cautious steps.

This wasn't supposed to happen. Zoe was supposed to be frozen, and Emma here with me. I was supposed to be...

I was alone with Zoe. I'd just signed my death warrant, whether I stayed in this box of a timeline or not.

On the other side of the wall, Zoe stopped pacing. Could she feel me here? Were Emma's powers active when we were frozen?

I took a deep breath. It was impossible to hide.

"Zoe."

"This was you?" she asked. More footsteps. "Yeah, it was. Why bring me in? How'd you bring me in?"

"It wasn't the plan."

"What was the plan?"

That was a hard one to answer, but she could read my mind either way. "To kill you before you hurt anyone else."

"So, Emma was a distraction."

"I prefer to think of myself as insurance." I felt the weight of the useless knife in my palm. "I don't think we thought we'd get this far."

"So, you figured you'd pause everything and stab me when I couldn't defend myself?"

I took another deep breath. There wasn't a good answer to that, was there? After a moment, I came around from my side of the wall, showing Zoe the knife in my hand but not letting go.

Maybe I should have just switched everything off, taken the chance that she'd smoked me in real-time. Reset and try again. Over and over until she was frozen, and I could do what I had to, but...

This could be the last chance to talk her down. Not that it had worked thus far.

"Yeah, that was the idea," I finally admitted.

"So, why're you on their side now?" she asked.

"Emma's side?" I suggested.

"Don't be difficult. I'm already being more patient than I need to be."

"I'm not on their side," I matched her implication. "I just want this to be over. I never wanted any of this to happen in the first place."

"You are, though."

"I'm not, Zoe."

"Toby, I've heard you think about it. You're not there yet, but you understand their points. You think you can solve these problems. You just hate that I'm the one in the way."

"I didn't mean to do this to you, Zoe."

"You didn't. They did."

"I brought you back," I said as I walked into the room proper. Several shards of wood were suspended in the air. I pushed them out of the way, but they stayed hanging once I let go. "Without me, none of this happens."

"Which part?" Zoe asked. "Just a matter of time until the hammer came down on these terrorists. Someone would realize they needed to go. All dying did was make it clear that it had to be me. That I'd been holding back for too long."

She was saying the words with perfect confidence, but somehow they didn't sound true.

"Where does it end?" I asked.

Zoe opened her mouth to speak but then took a second instead, then two, then three. Tick. Tick. Tick. She stared at the ground, then snapped her hand out at me.

I winced and braced, but nothing happened. When I opened my eyes, Zoe was still staring at the floor, but she'd clenched her hand into a fist.

"I...I don't know," she admitted. "It's so quiet here right now. I can hear myself think and..." She didn't need to finish the sentence for me to understand most of what she was trying to say. After a moment, she rallied her attention, wiping the glaze off her downward stare. "Just go."

"What?"

"Just leave now. Grab Emma, and get the hell out of here. Let me finish this, and then... you won't see me again until I've fixed it."

"You just said you don't know how it ends."

"Because I don't," she snapped. Zoe stomped the floor. I braced again, but nothing happened. Either Emma was still active, or she didn't have power here. "I don't know what fixes this. I don't know what's wrong. My head just keeps screaming at me to find them. To kill them. To finish this, but I don't know who they are!"

"Zoe."

"I beat Lexi, and it wasn't enough. I killed Kris, and it wasn't enough. I've hunted them down, and it wasn't enough. How many bodies, Toby? How many people am I going to kill before..." Zoe didn't trail off. She broke down, almost dropping to her knees before catching herself. "I'm not even there half the time. If I do anything other than hunt and kill, I'm just abandoned and alone! My power leaves me, and it's the one thing I have!" For the first time since the conversation began, I felt the licks of Zoe's power pricking against my skin. Testing me.

Shit.

"Just go. Get the hell out of here, and let me finish this, Toby."

"Is that a real offer?"

"Of course. I just need to take care of them and... and that'll fix it. If not, I'll figure it out. Or I'll die trying... Or..."

She left the opening, so I spoke up. "We walk away, and you'll just take care of all of them?" I motioned outside, and as I did, my grip on the knife slackened. Zoe was bruised. She was bleeding. She was panting. Was leaving really an option? Could I just get away with Emma at this point? Had we already done enough?

Would the two sides just burn each other out?

My hand was shaking. I grabbed my wrist to steady it. What was I doing with the knife? I wasn't a killer. Emma told me that. I knew that. This wasn't who I was. I couldn't do it again. I couldn't do it.

"Just this, and it's over?" I asked.

Zoe didn't meet my eyes as she lied. "Yes." Then, after a second, "I'm sorry you got caught up in this, Toby."

"Same."

"This was always my fight."

"Then..." There were so many things I wanted to say, but it was impossible to tell someone you wished you hadn't saved them. That they were dead instead of broken.

"Unfortunate reality." She said. I didn't know whether she was saying it to herself or answering my thoughts.

"Reality's unfortunate," I echoed. "We learn to live with it."

"You take Emma and go."

"Fine," I whispered, but she didn't need to read minds to understand it wasn't genuine. My grip loosened again, and the knife almost fell from my hand.

Zoe nodded.

I exhaled sharply, and time stuttered back into place.

The wall of the house was blown away, blood spread across the front lawn, and a discarded body was torn across it.

Zoe was in the room with me. A half dozen new cuts and bruises slashed across her face. She reached out a hand, and a man who'd been running in the other direction rose off the ground. Then screamed. Then stopped.

If we were leaving, we had to go now.

"Toby?" It was Emma behind me. Bruised. Discarded, but not broken. "What're you..."

I spun and then heard the splintering of bones behind me. Once I was in front of Emma, I bent down to help and draw her attention.

"You weren't supposed to be here," she said,

"I'm not an agent, suck at following orders." I winced as there was another scream behind me, just as I was getting a hand under the small of Emma's back to try to help her up. I glanced back to Zoe.

Emma caught it. "Toby, we can't stop her. I'm—"

"This is the part where I try." I'd just needed Emma to know my plan.

Zoe spun as she heard me. I blinked. She froze. Everything froze.

I ran past her outstretched hand and took her knife, shoving it into her exposed throat. I pulled my hands away as they began to shake. There wasn't any blood yet. That would only happen once everything started back up.

I wasn't ready to be a killer. I wasn't ready to do this.

But this had never been about what I was ready to do. It was about what I needed to do.

Time didn't snap back into motion; it bled. Wooded splinters cracking in the surrounding air. A wave of force pushed through the room. Emma's hand rose to meet Zoe's and protect us.

The seconds dripped by, and blood welled on Zoe's neck. Her

eyes struggled to focus on me, suddenly less than an arm's length away, and then they went wide as she realized what was happening.

The knife tore itself out of her throat, flying across the room and spraying blood out into the mix of dirt and drywall dust on the floor. Then blood poured from her neck, gushing out all at once like she'd been stabbed for ten seconds and did nothing about it.

Zoe screamed bloody murder into the sky. Half of her yell came out as her voice, and the other half came out as a garbled mess, trying to squeeze past the blood flowing from her throat. The ceiling above her trembled as she fell to her knees and then dropped forward. The scream didn't stop, and her power started to thrash around her. It kicked up rocks and debris as it raged. Like a god's tantrum, it cracked the floor before her and tore everything she could reach apart.

I took slow steps back as her blood-filled scream continued until she ran out of breath. After a few moments, the thrashing stopped, and the dirt stopped spraying. Zoe's power dripped away, just a second before she did.

The last second seemed to last a lifetime. In it, her pupils calmed, and her face unsnarled. There was something less manic about her in that final breath.

I reached out to try to stop everything for one last second. To avoid what I'd done. I wouldn't know if I'd brought her peace or just brought about the end.

I'd never get to know.

Time marched on.

Zoe lay still.

33

Second Dates

People celebrated when she fell, but I could see the missing pieces around us. Members of the Red calling out for each other. Most of them answered. Some didn't.

Emma and I were sitting on the splintered desk in the corner of the office, alone outside of the celebration. We didn't know these people. We'd come here to do what we had to do. We'd shown up as strangers, and we'd leave as strangers.

I would have rested my head in my hands, but there was blood on them.

"Toby," Emma said. By her tone, it was clear that it was the second or third time she'd called my name. How was I supposed to talk to her? I'd just killed her best friend. I'd killed Zoe. Maybe if I could have done something else. Maybe if one of us... "You okay?" she asked. She didn't look at me as she asked it; she was still staring into the space where it had all happened.

"Define okay."

"Surviving?"

"Then yeah." I looked over to her and offered a smile, but she wasn't looking at me. Her eyes almost glazed over during the gap in our conversation. I understood where she was coming from. We were both exhausted.

The silence went on too long, so I spoke up. "You?"

"I don't know."

"You don't know?"

"I'm not okay," she started, "but I was ready for it, you know."

"Yeah."

"At least I told myself I was." Emma swallowed nothing. I figured that we'd both expected tears in the end, but they hadn't showed. Dry throats and empty stares had taken their place.

"I'm sorry," I said.

"Why?"

"What?"

"Why are you sorry?" she asked.

"Well..." I almost didn't want to say it, but you couldn't get more real than the body in the room. "I killed Zoe."

"We did," Emma sighed, "but we didn't have a choice."

"I guess so."

"Fuck. Really, Emma, no tears?" she said to herself. She wiped the undersides of her eyes like she'd been crying, but she was just brushing the bags. "I cried like four times coming up to this, and now I'm here and..." Emma looked at me expectantly.

"Yeah?"

"Was it four?" Emma asked.

"Pardon?"

"I left the space there so you could correct me on how many times I cried before this," she said, "but now you ruined it." Emma leaned back, cracking her spine in several places. "I'd kill for a drink right now."

"Now?" I asked.

"I don't think there's a better time," Emma said.

"Well, I don't have one."

"Then you owe me one."

That gave me an idea. "Do you wanna start over?" I asked.

"What?"

"We can start over," I said. "Have another first date. I'm sure Todd and Soo will be down, you know, once they know we're alive."

"Just go on the first date again?"

"Well, I owe you a drink," I said. "Think about it. We can get rid of all the baggage," I said. "A fresh start."

Emma looked up at the cracked ceiling of the half-destroyed model home we were sitting in. She leaned against my shoulder, resting her head on me. I felt her hair tickling my neck. "Wanna know what?" she asked, then continued without letting me guess. "No."

"No?"

"No," Emma said. "This can already be the new beginning. We don't need to pretend it never happened."

"So, no second first date?" I asked.

"How about we make it to the second date first?" Emma asked, "And get you into therapy."

I almost argued for the sake of argument, but it would have looked really stupid while half-covered in drying blood. Instead, I coughed. We'd both swallowed so much dust.

A minute passed. Emma's breathing was steady and reassuring on my side.

"You two look surprisingly content," Lexi said as she walked up to us. She stared at the carnage for a moment before turning back.

"Shouldn't you be celebrating?" I asked.

"Before you turn yourself into the DPR," Emma continued for me.

"Yeah, yeah," Lexi sighed, "I'll do that. As for the celebrating? It's not the place or time for me right now. Someone's missing, right? And he would have loved to see this." Before either of us spoke up, she clarified, "us being safe, not specifically uh—"

"I get what you mean," I said after a moment.

"Thank you two," Lexi said. She tried to summon a soft smile alongside the thanks but couldn't quite manage it. Lexi nodded with that, slipping away from the pair of us to give us some space.

"What's after this?" I asked Emma once Lexi was out of earshot.

Emma pulled her phone out of her pocket and then frowned as the screen refused to turn on, the glass having caved in during the carnage.

I pulled out Todd's glacial antique. "What were you trying to look up?" I asked.

"The nearest nice hotel." Emma punched my shoulder. She was being playful, but I was a little too sore for it.

"Why?"

"A shower."

I snorted at that. "What about a date at the hotel bar after that?"

"Sure." Emma peeled her head off my shoulder, somewhat literally, considering the blood and sweat. "It took you long enough to ask me out on the second date, Toby."

"Hope it's worth the wait."

"It will be."

34

Epilogue

Callum Rehsman never returned as the head of the DPR, and in the first months following Zoe's fall, the Department had never followed up on Emma and my disappearance. Whether that was a courtesy was unclear.

After all, the fight over power regulation was a violent place, and people went missing all the time. What were two more ghosts in the system?

Emma got out of the driver's seat of the car first and cracked her neck. I heard the rattle climb most of the way up her spine.

"I could have driven for a bit, you know," I said as I unfolded myself out of the passenger seat. I'd been shoved up against the glove compartment for the sake of luggage space.

"Yeah, but this car is fun to drive so…" Emma took off her sunglasses and tucked them in the buttons of her blouse. "It was fine anyway."

"We beat the GPS by three hours," I said. Emma nodded but didn't look satisfied with the number.

I opened the trunk and pulled out the one suitcase that fit there. As I did, Emma stared up at the house, which my parents had painted robin's egg blue since I'd last seen it.

"You ready?" I asked once I'd rescued the suitcase that we'd stuffed in the backseat. We really hadn't been thinking about road trips when we bought the car.

"Could I ever be ready for something like this?" Emma asked.

"Emma Tavish, scared of a retirement community?"

"I'm not built for this kind of life."

"You're the one that wanted to come." I offered Emma her purse, and she accepted it.

"We had to come visit your parents."

"Yeah, well. We'll be here for a month," I said, "so get used to the pace of it."

Emma took a deep breath and clicked her tongue. Now that we'd been together for months, I knew that absolutely never meant anything good, but she didn't expound on what she'd meant by it.

I walked up to the door, and Emma followed a second later. She took another deep breath to steel herself, then grabbed my hand.

We rang the doorbell together. It was how we'd do everything.

Printed in Great Britain
by Amazon